# THE DEVY MAN

TRACY BROEMMER

The Devy Man

By

Tracy Broemmer

Horror Novella

Published by Tracy Broemmer

Edited by Lexie Broemmer

Cover by Redbird Designs

ISBN#: 978-1-951637-21-7

*For the little boy who first mentioned the devy man many, many years ago. I've been thinking about this all these years, and finally I wrote the story.*

# 1

From outside, the church looked more like a refurbished barn or a Morton building some farmer slapped up to handle the overflow of equipment. Some people even lived in buildings like that, but he knew it was a church. Oakboro Methodist. The new minister, Michael Tweedy, was young and progressive and as such, probably wouldn't last a week or two.

Moonlight washed out the gray building, making it shine white, almost ethereal. The steeple barely stood above the roof of the church, like a believer caught in a half stretch as he climbed from bed in the morning. Nothing compared to the steeple of St. James, the Catholic church twenty-seven miles down Highway 92, in the small town of Jester.

Catholics and Methodists shared some beliefs, Odell knew that, though he didn't know why he possessed that knowledge. He'd never been a church-going man, not since he was seven and his daddy walked out and Mama took to activities other than prayer that she could perform on her knees. Still, somehow, Odell knew.

Both religions believed in the Holy Trinity, that God is three persons: God the Father, God the son, and God the Holy Spirit. Both also believed in the Incarnation of Christ. In fact, only a minority of religions didn't believe that Jesus was the only begotten son of God, born of Mary. Odell knew about them, too. Christian Scientists. Islam. Jehovah's Witnesses, among others.

All that was neither here nor there to him.

Most of the cars were gone from the parking lot now, but he waited. Hidden from sight in the copse of trees south of the church, he'd watched the comings and goings all night. This wasn't about the faithful or faithfully departed, though he'd watched a lot of that, too. Odell found their rituals somewhat amusing, though if not for the hunt—if not for the task he'd been given—he would have tired of it by now.

The hymns grated on him, even at the distance he kept. Not so much the words, because even though he could hear everything—his hearing was sharper now, unlikely so, than when he was young—it was simply the atmosphere of worship that made him claw at his throat as if he might suffocate.

As if he could.

The minister—Michael Tweedy—like a five-year-old boy beaming with pride, wearing ridiculous bow ties and probably spit-shined black loafers, had the voice of an angel. Odell had spent the first few days listening to him from afar with his hands plastered over his ears and when he drew them away, he had not been surprised to see thick, black blood half congealed and dried on his palms.

Those surprises had scared the hell out of him at first, and then the hell had been put back in him, and now he feared nothing.

Still didn't love the church, but he had a job to do, and the church was the best place to do it.

He'd seen a wedding once, and the goodwill—both genuine and fake—made him ill. From his hiding spot in the woods, he had seen the groom and his men joshing in the gravel parking lot and he'd seen them pass a small bottle around and they each took a swig, and though Odell knew even the holiest sinned, he wondered what Reverend Michael Tweedy would say about that. They'd filed inside then, and Odell had watched with interest as the bride and her attendants gathered in nearly the same spot to whisper—they were joking about the wedding night, Odell heard every word—and giggle, and then they had wobbled across the gravel in their ridiculous heels, because slut attire was necessary for God to bless a marriage.

Odell had slumped against a giant oak tree when he heard the organist strike up Lohengrin's "Bridal Chorus," and in the shade while Bronwyn Smith promised her life to Hutch Montgomery, he closed his eyes and imagined a different sort of wedding night for the lovely couple. No sex for him anymore. No blood to rush anywhere, no electrifying jolts of sexual need. He could have unzipped his worn, almost colorless gray Dickies and wrapped his cold fingers around his shaft and yanked it off and not felt a thing.

Interesting thing was, thinking about blood and death aroused something entirely different in him. Made him feel alive, and imagining Hutch Montgomery wrapping his hands around his bride's throat to choke the life out of her when he mounted her whipped Odell into a frenzied state that made his dead heart pound so crazy hard, he'd had to climb to his feet and hunt for immediate gratification. He had long since stopped wondering how his weathered old fingers could catch prey, let alone snap a neck and decapitate a small animal. The smell of fresh blood always brought to mind the smell of his mama's house on Sunday mornings before Daddy left, back when she fixed Daddy a big breakfast. Those thoughts always gave way to visions of fire and blood, and Odell learned that those visions, the agony he perceived nourished his lifeless body nearly as much as the blood.

The first time he drank it, he licked the carcass clean, and then his dead stomach had cramped violently, and he'd fallen to his knees. The ground beneath him cold and wet, he'd dragged himself forward on all fours, long, yellowed nails digging for purchase in the fetid undergrowth beneath the canopy of trees. The vomit finally spewed from him, and then mouth sour and body shaking with exertion, his black soul awakened. Euphoria, unlike anything he'd ever known—even better than the times he'd forced himself on unsuspecting girls and women and copped a feel or tapped their gates of hell—had overcome him.

With that euphoria had come the knowledge. Flooding and painful at first, Odell had cowered in the woods. Had he been a praying man, he might have prayed a local find his body and call the coroner. The pressure in his head, the outrageous ache had grown until it peaked and erupted out of him in an unholy wail that he feared would draw attention.

No one had come.

The church had a large main gathering room and several smaller rooms used for storage and also for classes. There was a kitchen bigger than the tiny shack Odell had lived in after Mama was gone. Generic Merillat wooden cabinets probably purchased at the Home Depot in Jester and hung by Wilson and Son, the contractors here in Ivy. Some cabinets were bare; Odell was familiar with empty cabinets. Some had stacks of mismatched plates and soup bowls, the thick chunky plastic kind. There were a few stocked with staples like a government issued can of peanut butter, a box of cherry toaster pastries, and a box of generic cereal shaped like O's.

The restrooms were to the left of the kitchen when you entered the back door of the main room. The windows in the restrooms were frosted, but Odell paced the grounds often, and he was more than familiar with the layout. The church proper—the nave, where the congregation sat for services—was at the north end of the box-shaped building. Curiously, it was smaller than the community area with only two wide rows of fifteen straight-back wooden pews. No Communion rail separated the stark altar area from the nave. Only three red-carpeted stairs, and often, they—they being the reverend and his choir or the Ivy Preschool teachers—moved a set of homemade wooden risers to the altar.

No grand crucifix hung behind the table. Most Methodist churches didn't use a crucifix, though the Methodist symbol with the flame could use a cross or a crucifix. A wooden music stand stood at the right side of the altar and a small pulpit, the left. It, too, was unadorned and skinny enough that Reverend Tweedy couldn't get fidgety during a sermon without his congregation knowing it. The north end of Oakboro, where the nave and altar were, was directly under the small, white steeple.

Because there was no crucifix, Odell could go inside. While he feared nothing, it was the closest he came to feeling sheer discomfort. Anxiety pressed on his chest and drew beads of sweat to his greasy, clammy skin. But for the hunt, he could endure it.

Warm, yellow light glowed in a few of the windows. They wouldn't be using some of the side rooms tonight. But they had been in the nave, and now the stained-glass windows that depicted Jesus' life drew Odell's attention and his disgust. The community room was still lit, and now and then the back door—the heavy, industrial kind, not the pretty glass-paned doors of modern-day offices and shops—swung open, and someone carted out big cardboard boxes or garbage bags to toss in the oversized trash container.

From his hiding place, Odell watched each time, patiently waiting. The preschool teacher had already carried three boxes to her SUV, the one that sometimes wouldn't start. Phoenix Kelly, long and lithe and prime for the taking, had stood unafraid in the gravel lot and popped the hood of the SUV and poked around on more than one occasion. If Odell were able, he would have taken her. As it was, she would be a perfect steal. Lambs came in all shapes and sizes, and her long, lean calves—she wore skirts sometimes, which struck Odell as ridiculous—would be lustful in the air, thighs parted, and her breasts bared.

There would be blood, and maybe one day, there

would be time and true desire for that. Maybe if the hunt was successful, he would be given permission to rape and taste her before any sacrifice made. For now, Odell had a job to finish. He was parts anxious to complete the task and reluctant to move on. He didn't worry over what came next, but he wondered what it would be. This in-between period had been good; he was loathe to give up watching, though the excitement of nearing the end, of knowing he had the right one this time, was almost unbearable.

**2**

---

Halloween parties were just part of it. Part of childhood, of course. Phoenix Kelly still remembered the excitement of going to school on Halloween and counting down the seconds until the end of the learning day when their parties would start. Room mothers—usually two—would come in and lead the class in games. They played Halloween bingo with cards that read either *Trick* or *Treat*, they wrapped each other in toilet paper to see who could make the best mummy, and they were blindfolded and asked to touch things like cold spaghetti or sliced bananas to identify them. They were given treat bags and then sent home only to don their costumes and go out to trick or treat later and bring home more sugar.

Phoenix was on board with classroom parties. She had mothers who came in to help. They didn't really call them room mothers anymore, but then it had been years since she was in school and also, she had attended a Catholic grade school, and there was no question, there were differences in how things were done in private schools versus public schools. Seventeen four-year-olds made a lot of noise, and when you were having a Halloween party, they were that much louder. But Phoenix was okay with that; hard not to get caught up in the spirit of things when she was surrounded by the innocence and wonder of childhood. It would wear off soon she knew; in fact, several of her students had older siblings and sure enough, those students wanted everything to be gory and scary instead of fun and adventurous.

She was okay with the parades, too, though something about it this year felt creepy. She knew it was stupid, because for one thing, the only real thing about Halloween—as far as she was concerned—was the sugar high every kid she taught would reach before the night was over.

Ross Harvey banged into the kitchen again carrying one of the large black trash cans from the community room. She glanced at him over her shoulder as she rinsed the last bowl and set it gently in the sink. The chunky plastic wouldn't break if she winged it at the wall, but she was exhausted, her head was beginning to pound, and she wanted silence. Pipe dream, as long as Ross and Lynnea were around.

Was Lynnea still here? She hadn't seen her at all in the past fifteen minutes.

"It's gettin' cold out there," Ross grumbled. Phoenix offered him a tired smile. She liked him, but she was reluctant to get caught up in a long conversation. As soon as she finished her checklist of to-do items, she was out of here. The twenty-three-minute drive home would give her ample time to decompress after all the giggling and squealing that had gone on this evening. Once home, she planned to pour a glass of wine—the good stuff, not the bottled sugary stuff given to her by one of her kids' moms—undress, and climb into a hot bath where she would further decompress after the entire month of October with a classroom full of four-year-old children.

She shuddered to think of what came next. Thanksgiving—believe it or not, it was a big thing in preschool. Christmas—except they couldn't call it that. Winter break. Winter holidays. But not Christmas.

Phoenix rolled her eyes as she turned back to the sink.

"Where did Lynnea go?" Ross asked as he dragged the trash can closer to her. Phoenix flinched at the ripe smell and wondered yet again why he didn't just leave the can in place and empty the full bags out and then put a new one in.

"I don't know." She shrugged and then covered a yawn. "Maybe she left."

"Car's out there," he mumbled absently.

Phoenix didn't really believe Lynnea would just leave without saying anything, but now she was concerned. "Was she feeling okay?"

"Far as I know."

Five feet eight, Ross wasn't much taller than Phoenix. She watched him struggle to reach the box of trash bags high in the corner cabinet.

"Why don't you just move them?" she suggested for the hundredth time.

"I do." He finally snagged the box and pulled it down.

"Trust me, do you think I want you to watch me fail at something so basic?"

She snorted when he looked up at her. Maybe he wasn't a big guy, but he was easy on the eyes. And nice. And married. Phoenix knew his wife, though she didn't know her well. They owned the little white cottage on the corner of the main drag and Seventh. His wife, Beth, was pregnant with their first baby, and though Ross was the caretaker of the church and already good friends with Reverend Tweedy, Phoenix often told him to let her finish things and get home to Beth.

"Somebody keeps putting them back up there on that shelf."

"I don't know anyone around here that tall," Phoenix said with a soft laugh. "Go home, Ross. I'll finish up."

"Nope, I'm good."

"Seriously." She exchanged the scratch pad for a dishtowel and started drying the dishes they had used tonight. "All I have to do is finish these and then turn the lights out and go."

"And find Lynnea," he reminded her. "And you still have kids here."

"What?" She jerked her chin around in his direction, giving him her complete attention.

"Charlie Baker and Anthony Hale."

"Are you kidding—? What're they doing?" In her haste to check on the kids, she crashed the bowl on the counter and jumped at the noise it made. Ross tugged a plastic bag from the box and shook it out.

"Anthony's drawing something," he told her. "And Charlie's staring at the wall."

Sadly, that sounded about right. Phoenix sighed and tossed the dishtowel down. "You can go, Ross. Really."

"Beth's fine," he said quietly. "Her sister's with her. I'll lock up and walk you out."

Phoenix bristled as she hurried out of the kitchen. She didn't need Ross to walk her out. She didn't need Ross or anyone else to do anything for her. At twenty-nine, she had lived enough to be fiercely independent and proud of it. Still, Ross was just that kind of guy, and rather than take offense, maybe she should be grateful guys—people—like that still existed.

Besides, if she were honest with herself, she would admit she had been uncomfortable since the parade this morning. Earlier, she had written it off as the chill in the air and the fact that she hadn't worn a heavy coat, and she had to march her preschoolers down Gates over to Bristow and back in the drizzle. Kind of felt like something more, but she couldn't put her finger on it. She'd had that feeling all day that someone was watching her, but then by definition, a parade was an ostentatious display, and yes, people in town had come out to watch them.

Wondering again where her assistant was, Phoenix glanced to her left as she left the kitchen. The hall was well lit, but the restrooms appeared to be dark. Had she sent Lynnea on an errand and forgotten? Entirely possible. Phoenix was so ridiculously tired; she could probably lay down on the institutional gray and green carpet and sleep until morning. She trailed her fingers over the water table—since it was fall, it currently held dried leaves rather than water—and looked over the small play kitchen on the opposite wall. One of the kids had left play dishes in the sink. With a sigh, she started to remedy that, but she remembered that Charlie and Anthony were still here.

First priority was to get the kids taken care of. In this case, that meant get the kids home. And then she could finish tidying up and go home. Her class met only three days a week, so her weekend sort of started now. Granted, she would be working on lesson plans and gathering new learning materials, and she needed to make some notes for grading. The Ivy Preschool used a noncompetitive grading system, so Phoenix never gave letter grades or percentages. She didn't pass or fail kids, either. Rather, she documented their progress in skill areas important to child development. She made written notes, and she saved photographs of the kids, as well as their own work, and she did occasional state mandated testing as well.

Still, even with all of those things to do tomorrow and Friday, with no kids around it would feel more like a weekend. But first, she had to take care of Charlie and Anthony. Phoenix loved kids. She'd carried one once, for three months and lost it and the baby's father, and since then, she hadn't allowed herself the time it took to get to know anyone enough to be involved or to love him. True, women her age and older had babies every day, and when asked—people in Ivy were bold and rude enough to ask and ask often—if she was ever going to have a kid, she would simply smile and offer a shrug and a *maybe someday*.

After teaching full time for six years and working part time for just over a year before that as a substitute, she figured she'd seen it all. Kids with the best family circumstances, in good health, financially sound, and genuinely happy. Kids with divorced parents and kids who had never known at least one of their parents. Kids with learning disorders and kids with physical disabilities. She'd sat side by side with a little girl who commandeered her mother's Chanel perfume every morning and with a little girl who smelled and looked as if she only bathed twice a week.

Phoenix taught a high school history class for a few weeks while a teacher recovered from surgery. In that room, she had encountered a student with a drinking problem, and she'd overheard a few boys whispering about stealing a car. She loved them all.

But something about Anthony Hale niggled at her. Probably the big brown eyes framed in the long thick lashes women paid big money for. He was poor in every sense of the word, and dirty didn't describe only his blond hair, but everything from his face down to his socks.

"You guys, what are you still doing here?" She infused her voice with the expected exuberance for preschool teachers, but it didn't rouse either of the boys. Anthony, his whole upper body draped over the tabletop, continued to sing quietly as he drew yet another picture. Anthony without a pencil or crayon in his hand was like a guitar without strings.

Phoenix, aware of Ross banging around in the kitchen, glanced at the big watch face on her left wrist. It was nearly nine. The Halloween program—yes, *program* and Phoenix thought mandating a Halloween program was a bit over the top—had ended two hours ago. The social hour for the children with their parents and grandparents and aunts and uncles and whatever had wrapped up almost an hour ago. She stood for a moment at the table, just behind Anthony, but both boys remained oblivious to her presence.

Charlie Baker gave her the creeps.

She flinched, guilt clutching her belly with hard, bony fingers, and giving it a vicious twist. The kid had always been different, but over the past few weeks, he had gone total freak on her. Lynnea refused to talk to him. Phoenix swallowed the revulsion and stepped around the table, smoothing her fingertips over Anthony's shoulder as she did so. His only response was a deep, wet sniffle. Knowing he'd just swallowed a mouthful of snot made Phoenix hesitate, but she reminded herself this was her job. *All the glamour.*

Maybe when she got home, she would stand under a scalding hot shower for fifteen or twenty minutes and then have a glass of wine.

"Charlie." She touched the kid's shoulder, gave it a gentle squeeze. He remained frozen, his shoulder stiff and ungiving. Had his family been here earlier? She lowered herself to sit in the tiny red plastic chair at the table next to him and tried to meet his eyes. Used to be this kid didn't stop talking; sometimes Phoenix worried he wasn't breathing, he talked so much. He was rough and mean, and he talked about older girls in words that Phoenix wanted to believe he didn't understand. But he lived with his dad, and he had an older brother in junior high, and so she feared he knew more than most four-year-olds.

His dad had been here. Phoenix remembered seeing Tom Baker with a girl who looked younger than herself. It wasn't her job to judge, and mostly, Phoenix remembered that. But it was hard not to when something had a direct, negative effect on one of her kids. Charlie Baker needed his mother, and if he couldn't have her—he couldn't, because she'd passed away of cancer when he was two— he needed his father. Not half a father and a slew of his dad's girlfriends who wanted to mother him and hook up with his daddy. The guy wasn't bad looking, and Phoenix liked him well enough. She just wished he would try a little harder. Maybe it was too late to keep his older son Quentin out of trouble, but there was time to steer Charlie in the right direction.

Silence.

Well, no, that wasn't true. Anthony was half humming and singing, and Ross was still clanging stuff around in the kitchen—Phoenix had no idea what he was doing, but he worked for the church, not the preschool who only rented space in the church, so for all she knew, he had been told to polish the linoleum floors in the kitchen and bathrooms. Charlie stared unblinking at the heavy retractable curtain that cordoned off the nave of the church from the community room where they sat.

His grandparents had been here, too, Phoenix was startled to realize. She had talked to Vivian Baker. How had they forgotten to take him when they left? *Who did that?* Phoenix heard Ross' quick footsteps now as he headed to the back door. She sat still, eyes on Charlie, and listened to the bang of the metal door on the frame as it closed.

The Halloween program had been the first ever. And though Phoenix had rolled her eyes when her supervisor handed the order down, she had to admit now that it had been fun. The kids, dressed in costume, had stood on the risers in the church and sang five cute little Halloween songs and chants, like *Five Little Pumpkins*. Nothing like seventeen four-year-olds dressed like Optimus Prime and Jason from *Friday the 13<sup>th</sup>* and a ninja and cheerleaders and pirates gathered in a church singing about pumpkins and witches.

Anthony wasn't humming anything they had performed for their families, though. Phoenix recognized it, but she found herself leaning around Charlie to hear him better. Charlie didn't flinch at her nearness; it was as if he was in a catatonic state. Phoenix swallowed a mouthful of unease as she strained to hear what Anthony was singing.

The tune was "Aikendrum." But he was saying the words wrong.

Phoenix looked around the community room again. The lights were still on, though the small side rooms were dark. The Halloween decorations were of the cute variety, rather than creepy, being that they were in a church and the kids were preschoolers. Still, the stare of the skeleton hanging on the back of the nearly closed door directly across from her—the quilting room, though it was so tiny, Phoenix doubted one woman and one quilt project would fit inside—was beginning to bug her.

"Lynnea?" she called. Her voice betrayed her exhaustion. She had to get these boys home. She would worry about putting the dishes away and tidying up the play areas tomorrow. The Halloween decorations could wait until tomorrow, too. Pain radiated up her stiffening neck into the back of her head, and her legs hurt from kneeling in front of the risers earlier to direct the kids. Which really meant keeping them corralled.

When there was no answer, Phoenix looked back at Charlie. He hadn't moved. She let her eyes move over him slowly, cataloging his Spiderman costume, his long, skinny fingers with fingernails that should have been trimmed a week ago. Under the costume, she could see the collar of a blue T-shirt, and on his legs, navy sweatpants peeked out from under the costume. His feet—clad in worn, generic white tennis shoes—were piled one on top of the other. She stared at his body long enough to see the shallow movement of his shoulders, the slightest rise and fall of his chest to ensure that he was breathing.

Anthony sang a few mumbled words, and again, Phoenix could make out the tune of "Aikendrum."

Lynnea hadn't answered her, but at the moment, Phoenix was more concerned about the boys. It really shouldn't be that much of a surprise, she supposed, that they were still here. Anthony's parents were often late, terribly late, picking him up from school in the daytime, not to mention all the missed home visits Phoenix had to reschedule. This was sort of par for the course. And now that she thought about it, she wasn't sure she had seen anyone in Anthony's family here earlier tonight. Guilt stabbed at her again; she should know for certain if his family had been here. That was as much a part of her job as teaching.

Still, the more curious situation was that Charlie Baker's family had been here—including his grandmother —and though his dad was maybe somewhat less than responsible, he wasn't a bad guy. Phoenix wondered if maybe Tom had slipped back into the nave of the church for some quiet time. Maybe he had asked Charlie to wait in the community room. That would make sense. Tom and Sheila used to be religious; Phoenix had learned that from Vivian. As was sometimes the case after losing a loved one, he had lost his faith and his way, hence the lack of parenting skills and the influx of young girls.

Praying this was it, that she would find one of the Baker family in the nave, she moved quickly to the main door of the community room. The retractable curtain had a snap closure, and Phoenix didn't care to struggle with the snap mechanism now. She stepped into the small foyer of the building, glanced out the glass pane by the front door and noticed Lynnea's car, and then turned her attention to the church proper. Disappointment stole in when she saw darkness through the glass pane in that door, but just in case there was a Baker praying in the dark, she pulled the wooden door open and stepped inside.

Usually, the still hush in a church—any church—was a comfort to her. Tonight, though, Phoenix was on edge and ready to go home. Leaving the door open, she stepped away and then changed her mind and went back. She would prop the door open, never mind that she had no intention of being in here for a total of two minutes. She'd seen enough horror movies to know that door could close suddenly and lock her inside. In the light of the foyer, she looked around and nudged her foot around for the doorstop. Frustrated when she didn't find it, she squatted down and patted the carpeted floor behind the door.

"This is stupid," she mumbled. "Turn the light on, Phoenix."

Since she was already squatting at the door and because she knew there was a doorstop around some-where, she stayed where she was, left hand holding onto the door, right patting the floor in search of the rubber stop. Her fingers brushed something furry, drawing a sharp squeal of terror before she remembered the church had a mouse problem.

She gave up on finding the doorstop when her stomach heaved. She climbed to her feet, fisting her fingers and then straightening them over and over, and nearly tripped around the door. Left hand sliding over the wall, she tried to slow her breathing as she searched now for the light switch.

Which was *gone? What?*

She gulped down another panicked squeal. No need to scare the boys in the next room. But, still, she smoothed her hand over the wall again. No switch.

"What the—?" Phoenix wasn't a prude; in fact, when not around seventeen four-year-olds, she had the mouth of a sailor. The boys were too far away to hear her, but it felt wrong to cuss in the church, so she bit her tongue and then remembered the light switches were on the other side of the door. Combination of poor planning on the contractor and electrician's part and the fact that she really didn't have much reason to ever be in the actual church.

"You okay?"

She jumped when Ross spoke just outside the door.

"Heard you scream."

"I didn't scream," she mumbled indignantly. "I squealed."

"Right." He nodded, though Phoenix saw the look of amusement on his face. "What's up?"

"Dead mouse."

"Mm." He grimaced. "Let me get gloves, and I'll get it. What're you doing in here?"

"I was hoping Charlie's dad or grandma had ducked in

for a quick prayer." She shrugged and looked over her shoulder to find the room empty. "I don't know how you forget a kid."

"What about Anthony?"

"Whole other story," she mumbled, but she bit her tongue. She couldn't discuss any of the kids with anyone outside of family. Even if everyone she spoke to here in Ivy knew the kids and their families better than she did. "But I'm not even sure he had anyone here tonight."

"Jovi brought him," Ross told her. "Dropped him off at the door."

Sixteen-year-old sisters wouldn't be interested in staying for a preschool sibling's Halloween program. Phoenix understood that. But the family should have made plans for who would pick Anthony up when the evening was over.

"Okay." Phoenix sighed. "I'll call parents. See what's going on."

Leaving the door open and the lights on for Ross to dispose of the dead mouse, Phoenix went back to the community room. Neither of the boys had moved. Anthony had stopped humming, though, so the only sound in the room was the low buzz of the lights that Phoenix had grown used to after the first month of teaching there.

"Hang on, guys," she announced as she walked by the table where they sat. She dug through her purse—open on her desktop—and pulled her cell phone from it. She would call Tom Baker first; he was easier to deal with than Anthony's parents.

She touched her phone screen and remembered she needed to wash her hands.

"I'm gonna go wash my hands, guys. Be right back."

Charlie hitched his chin; the sudden movement startled her. She had a smile ready for him, but when he turned his vacant stare to her, she noticed a drop of dark —almost black—blood under his left nostril.

## 3

Nosebleeds didn't scare her. Vomit didn't scare her. Open wounds gushing blood didn't scare her. She had been teaching too many years to lose her cool over any of the above. Tonight, the one drop of dark blood under Charlie's nose unnerved her. Because it wasn't the first time. It had happened first two days ago. Monday morning.

He had come to school with pasty-white skin and blood red lips like he was dressed as a vampire for Halloween. Five days early. Phoenix had dropped her hands gently on his shoulders to steer him away from the cubbies where the children hung their coats and backpacks. Assuming he had the stomach flu that was currently making its way around the grade school a few blocks away, she had pressed the back of her hand to his cheek. Finding his skin cold and dry, she'd moved her hand up over his forehead, only to decide he didn't have a fever. Before she could send him back to the cubbies, she noticed a drop of dark blood just under his left nostril.

Normally talkative, and sometimes much too loud, Charlie hadn't said a word Monday. Or all week, for that matter.

Phoenix tossed her phone down on her desk now and moved back to stand by the boy. She didn't like his usual attitude, but right now she would welcome it. He stared at her now as lifelessly as he had stared at the curtain before when she had sat with him and Anthony.

"Charlie?" she said quietly. "Are you okay?"

No answer. No head shake yes or no. No indication that he even heard her speaking to him. Her legs protested when she squatted down in front of him, but she balanced there and studied his face. He had moved with her, tilted his chin and his head to watch her, but his eyes were still vacant. Phoenix suppressed a shiver. Aware that she still hadn't washed her hands, she didn't want to touch him. But she needed to make sure he was okay.

"Come with me, okay, buddy?" Impressed to sound calm, she stood slowly and reached for Charlie, stopping just short of touching his arm with her left hand. "Let's get a tissue, and I need to wash my hands."

He stood to follow her, but he said nothing. Phoenix tried to remember if he had participated in the program. Had he been singing? Even boys were enthusiastic about school programs when they were four. But had *he* joined in earlier? She did a mental run through of each song they'd sung, trying to picture each child's face as she did so.

No. She was pretty sure Charlie hadn't opened his mouth tonight.

"Anthony, we'll be right back, okay?" She glanced

down at the other boy, surprised and pleased when he looked up at her with a warm smile.

"Okay, Miss Phoenix."

Buoyed by the response, Phoenix leaned in to look at Anthony's drawing. She could make out a tree and some sort of animal. Normally, she would sit down and ask what he was drawing, but right now she wanted to wash her hands and take care of Charlie.

She started walking, relieved when Charlie fell into step beside her. He was tall and lanky for his age, all arms and legs. His platinum blond hair was uneven, as if he had taken a scissors to it himself. Phoenix snuck a peek at him as they neared the kitchen. She noticed another drop of blood at his other nostril.

"Charlie, have you had nosebleeds at home this week?" she asked as she led the boy into the kitchen. He stood near her when she washed her hands, but he stared back toward the community room, where they could see Anthony through a giant window in the wall. Anthony tapped the eraser end of his fat pencil on the table, eyes glued to the west wall above Phoenix's desk.

She scrubbed her hands nearly raw under scalding water, gagging at the tactile memory of the dead mouse.

"Hey. Ross said you were looking for me." Lynnea appeared in the kitchen suddenly, looking out of breath and a bit harried.

"Hey." Phoenix dried her hands and then yanked two latex gloves from a small box on the counter and looked at Lynnea. "Where were you?"

"I walked out with Dru Kraft and her parents." She rolled her eyes. "Sandy was asking me about Dru's behavior."

Phoenix grinned, but because they weren't alone, she didn't say anything. Dru was an adorable little girl with big brown eyes and fangs. The kid was mean as a snake; she would throw anyone under a bus to get her way.

"There was an accident out on the highway," Lynnea continued. "Sandy and I walked over to see what was going on."

"What was Mike doing?" Phoenix asked about Dru's father.

"He was on the phone. Stayed at the car with Dru."

Phoenix rolled her eyes now. "Anybody hurt? In the accident?"

"Yeah." Lynnea yawned now. "You didn't hear the sirens?"

"Nope. All I've heard is Anthony humming 'Aikendrum.'"

"He's still here, too?"

Phoenix hitched her chin at the window, suggesting Lynnea take a look.

"Oh wow." She frowned and rolled her head on her neck. "What a night."

"So, how bad?"

"Took Carter Darby to the ER. Looked pretty bad. He wasn't moving."

Phoenix flinched. Remembering that Charlie was in the room with them, she turned her attention to him and bit down on the rest of the questions she wanted to ask. Without looking, she snatched two tissues from the box on the big table and put them up to the boy's nose.

"Another nosebleed?" Lynnea groaned. "Poor Charlie."

"Poor Carter," Phoenix mumbled.

"Dixon Harrison." Lynnea's reverent tone drew Phoenix's attention.

"He was with Carter?"

Lynnea nodded. She dropped her gaze to Charlie and then looked back at Phoenix with big eyes.

"Oh, no." Phoenix swallowed hard. Her eyes burned with tears, but she refused to cry here in front of any of the kids.

"Second big accident this month," Lynnea mumbled.

Phoenix nodded as she pulled the tissue away from Charlie's face. She had removed most of the blood under his nose, just a spot of red remained. The other accident hadn't been fatal, but bad enough. Shaun Petry had wrecked his four-wheeler in the woods; his girlfriend had walked away with a few scratches, but Shaun had taken a trip to the ER and come home with a cast on his arm and fourteen stitches in his face.

"Did you call Tom?" Lynnea asked her.

"Started to." She shook her head, too tired to share the whole story.

"I'll do it," Lynnea announced.

"Thanks."

"I can take Charlie on my way," Lynnea told her. "If it's necessary."

Phoenix didn't like to do that; she didn't like having the kids in their personal cars because of liability issues. The trouble was after working in Ivy as long as she had, she had developed friendships with family members, so small favors, such as taking a student home, weren't a big deal.

Except this felt different.

This was a nighttime event, and Charlie's family had been here, and they'd left him here.

"Feelin' okay?" she asked Charlie, not expecting an answer.

"My head hurts." His voice was scratchy, as if he hadn't spoken in days.

"I think Daddy needs to take you to the doctor," she mumbled absently.

"I can't." Charlie shook his head almost violently.

"What do you mean?"

"He said I can't go to the doctor."

"Daddy said that?"

"No. The man did."

"What man, Charlie?" Phoenix watched his face as she peeled the latex gloves off. She balled the bloody tissues up in the gloves and tossed all of it in the trash under the sink. Charlie scratched at his head absently. Phoenix glanced at his fingers in his hair and wondered if he had lice. She hadn't seen him digging earlier; come to think of it, she hadn't seen Charlie move much at all this week.

"Tom said he was in the backseat of the car," Lynnea told her as she moseyed back into the kitchen.

"What?"

"Right?" Lynnea shrugged. "Why is Anthony singing 'Aikendrum' when the rest of the kids are stuck on 'Five Little Pumpkins'?"

Phoenix gave Lynnea a dramatic eyebrow shrug and laughed softly. "Why is grass green?"

"It's not," Charlie answered. Phoenix looked at him again, but he was back to staring at the floor as if he were in a trance.

"Will you call Dennis Hale? If we get Anthony taken care of, I'll drive Charlie home. I want to talk to Tom."

"Sure." Lynnea nodded, eyes already on the phone in her hand.

"Charlie, were you in Daddy's car?"

No answer.

"Why did you get back out?"

"I thought I heard him."

"You thought you heard who?" Phoenix coaxed him. "Daddy?"

Charlie nodded absently, but he mumbled something about *the man*.

"What did he say?"

"To get out."

Phoenix smacked her lips together and drew in a slow, deep breath. She heard Lynnea do the same behind her. Charlie blinked at the floor, his concentration drawing her attention to a drop of blood near the boy's feet. She had no idea what Charlie heard earlier, but she was certain Tom Baker hadn't collected his family to go home and then told Charlie to get out of the car.

Assuming she had missed the drop of blood moments ago when she was talking to Lynnea, she moved to grab a paper towel from the dispenser on the counter.

"Miss Phoenix?" Charlie whispered.

"Jovi?" Lynnea said behind her. Relieved that Lynnea had made contact with someone in the Hale household, she wetted a small portion of the towel and then turned back to wipe up the spot.

"Oh! Charlie!" she yelped when she realized bright red blood was now gushing from his nose. "Hang on, hon."

The paper towel and the spot on the floor forgotten,

Phoenix pulled two more latex gloves from the open box on the counter and snapped them over her hands. Lynnea had stepped out of the kitchen, but Phoenix could still hear her speaking. She said a quick prayer that Jovi or one of Anthony's other siblings, or parents for that matter, would get here quickly to pick him up, and then she turned her full attention back to Charlie.

"Here." Phoenix lifted Charlie's hands to cup them around a wad of tissues at the tip of his nose. "Tilt your head back. C'mere." She stretched to the far right and pulled a chair out for him and then nudged him into it.

"What's wrong with Charlie, Miss Phoenix?"

"Just a nosebleed, Anthony," she replied calmly. "Nothing to worry about."

She looked up for Anthony, but he was still seated out in the community room, draped over his drawing again. Phoenix blinked, certain that he had just been standing in the kitchen. Someone with his voice most definitely just asked about Charlie, but there's no way she would have heard him so clearly if he were sitting out there. No way he could have moved that quickly back to his seat, either.

"Lynnea?" she called. She was anxious to know if her assistant got anything out of Jovi, like if anyone was on his or her way to pick Anthony up.

"Dennis is on his way." Lynnea strode into the room, talking as she moved. "Jovi said she had a date, but when she left to bring Anthony here, she thought Dennis was picking him up. Dennis says he fell asleep."

"Is he sober?" Phoenix asked quietly, no longer particularly concerned about Charlie overhearing their conversation. This night had gone on far too long, and things were just a little too weird to worry about filtering their conversation now.

"I dunno." Lynnea shook her head. "He sounded out of it, like it's totally possible Jovi woke him up to take my call."

Phoenix nodded. "What about Tom? Is he coming back?"

"He asked if one of us could bring Charlie home."

"Of course, he did," Phoenix mumbled. "And what about Ross? Is he still here?"

"He was out back a few minutes ago. Something about dead animals."

"I found a dead mouse in the church."

"No, he said animals. Like a pile of them out at the edge of the lot."

Phoenix held her breath and counted to three. "Awesome."

"Want me to drive Charlie? Or wait with Anthony?"

"Why don't you go on home?" Phoenix suggested. "I'll wait with Anthony, and then I can take Charlie. I need to speak with Tom about these nosebleeds."

"I can wait with you," Lynnea offered and shook her head. "I'd rather not walk out alone."

Phoenix wouldn't admit it, but she understood what Lynnea was feeling. She was spooked, too, and walking outside into the dark parking lot—one light propped on the back of the church building didn't do much to fight a whole county of darkness—after the weird stuff happening was the last thing she wanted to do alone.

"Okay." She gave in and met Lynnea's eyes with a nod. They shared a grin.

"I could go for a marg right about now." Lynnea set her

phone on the counter and then hopped up to sit beside it. Phoenix nodded, but she peeked at Charlie to see if he reacted to Lynnea's word choice. She would very much like a margarita right now, maybe a pitcher of them.

"Right?"

"Tyler Camden."

Phoenix yanked her gaze from the window at Lynnea's back where she had been watching Anthony to look Lynnea in the eyes.

"What about him?"

The way the night was going, Phoenix wondered if the kid had just come inside the building via the back door. Maybe before the night was over, all seventeen of their preschoolers would inexplicably be back in the classroom.

"He had a nosebleed last week," Lynnea reminded her.

Phoenix tipped her head at Lynnea's words. To hide her frustration—she should have remembered that—she leaned over Charlie and pulled gently on his hands to check the tissues under his nose. Though there was some blood in the tissues, the bleeding appeared to have stopped. For now, anyway.

"Not like that, but he had that one dark drop of blood. Remember?"

"I do," Phoenix said quietly. "That's really weird. I mean, nosebleeds aren't contagious."

"Huh-uh." Lynnea shook her head. "Unless it's just the weather. The air's been dry. I heard the sheriff's been warning people out in the boonies not to burn anything right now. The woods at the edge of town could go up in flames."

Charlie mumbled something that sounded like *fire*. Phoenix was a little startled to think he might be paying attention to their conversation and a little bit relieved, too. She also had to bite her lip to keep her thoughts to herself, because in her opinion, there wasn't much more to the town of Ivy than the boonies.

"Maybe." She shrugged and then added, "probably." Because that had to be the only explanation. Still, she worried it might be an indication of a cold or a sinus infection coming on, so she did want to talk to Charlie's father.

"It's not even Halloween yet." Lynnea sounded miserable.

Phoenix laughed softly, but the sound froze in her throat when she looked over Lynnea's shoulder through the window and didn't see Anthony.

"What?" Lynnea jumped down immediately. She turned to see what Phoenix was looking at and was halfway out of the kitchen before Phoenix could move. "Anthony?"

"Charlie, stay right there, okay?" Phoenix went out the door on the opposite side of the room and swept the hallway as she had done earlier when she was looking for Lynnea. "Lynn, is the door locked up front?"

"I flipped it when I came inside," Lynnea answered from the heart of the community room.

"Call Jovi. See if Dennis left yet. I'm gonna peek outside for Ross."

She'd never lost a child. Well, she'd never lost a child that wasn't hers in a classroom. Heart in her throat—though she reminded herself to stay calm—she moved back through the hall to the bathroom to check for Anthony. She peeked her head inside the women's room first, flipped the light on, but the two stall doors were open, and the room was empty. Still, what if for some crazy reason Anthony had snuck in here and climbed on a toilet to hide from them?

She went inside and checked both stalls only to find them both empty. A flash of movement to her left caught her attention when she turned around. Terror seized her lungs—not like touching the dead mouse earlier but worry that someone had come in to take Anthony—but when she looked to her left, she saw only her own reflection in the rectangular mirror over the two sinks. She looked harried; the loosed curls from her messy bun made her look crazy. She rushed out of the room without giving it another thought—who had time to worry about messy hair and wild eyes at a time like this?

The same check in the men's room produced the same results. Although this time, she was prepared for her reflection in the mirror. Just not the bloody fingerprint on the back of the sink. Had Charlie come in here? Before she noticed his bloody nose? Or had he wandered in and out of the men's room while she was checking the ladies' room?

Phoenix left the light on as she darted out of the men's room and back to the kitchen. Charlie hadn't moved. He sat at the table, tissues pressed to his nose, still as a statue. Satisfied that he was okay, that he was safe, Phoenix slipped back out to the community room praying that she would find Lynnea sitting with Anthony at the table.

No such luck. No one was around. But she heard humming as she loped across the room and to the right to the back of the building. Lynnea must have gone outside to search for Anthony. Phoenix hit the bars on the door hard and pushed it open in a rush. At the back of the property line, Ross jerked his head up in surprise and looked at her.

"Everything okay?" he called.

Phoenix wanted to jog out to him to investigate this dead animal business. What if one of the high school boys was messing with her and Lynnea? Or with the kiddos here? But she didn't have time to worry about it now, and she refused to wander that far from the building with Charlie alone inside.

"Did you see Dennis Hale?"

"Haven't seen him all night," Ross answered. He turned to face her, hands at his sides. Phoenix could tell he was wearing thick work gloves. Her stomach soured at the worry over the dead animals. What kinds of animals? Dead how? she wondered.

"Just now? You didn't see his truck?"

"No." In the shadows at the far end of the lot, Ross shrugged helplessly. "Why? What's going on?" He stepped over something—Phoenix didn't care to think too hard about what—and trotted over to her.

"We can't find Anthony."

"What?"

"Lynnea and I were in the kitchen with Charlie. He had a nosebleed. Anthony was there one second and then he was gone."

"Was Dennis coming to get him?"

"Supposedly." Phoenix groaned. "Dammit, we need more light in this lot."

"Phoenix, maybe he pulled in and out, and I didn't realize it. But I sure didn't hear anything."

"Okay."

"What about Charlie? Is Tom coming back for him?"

"I'm gonna drive him home after we take care of Anthony."

"Okay. I was bagging up the...." Ross gestured wildly over his shoulder. "Remains. But I'll start looking for Anthony."

"Thank you." Phoenix nodded. "Um. Lynnea called Jovi back. And she's looking for Anthony. I'll see if she got a hold of Jovi."

Ross turned on his heel and hollered for Anthony as Phoenix went back inside. Fearing the worst, she hustled back to the kitchen and nearly wept with relief when she found Charlie, his head cradled on his arms at the table.

"Charlie, Charlie, Charlie." She sighed as she crossed the room on trembling knees. The bloodied tissues were half falling from his hand. Eyes closed, his shoulders moved up and down in a steady, deep rhythm. Just to be on the safe side, Phoenix touched his cheek with the back of her hand. Cool and dry.

"Phoenix?" Lynnea called. Her voice came from the back of the building. Phoenix hurried back to the doorway to meet her in the hall. "Jovi said Dennis just left."

"Dammit," Phoenix groaned. She clutched her stomach, though everything in her body felt wrong. The whole night had been such a weird mishmash of stuff, and the thought of dead animals piled out back for the kids to find made her want to vomit. But the fear, the nightmare of losing a child, was terrifying. That it was actually happening was that much worse.

"I didn't see Anthony. Just told Ross that Dennis just left to come here. I'm goin' back out with Ross."

"You stay with Charlie." Phoenix shook her head. "I should go out there."

"You look like you're gonna pass out," Lynnea argued.

"Charlie's sleeping," Phoenix ignored Lynnea's comment. "Let me just go take a look. I can't just sit here, Lynn."

"He's not sleeping." Lynnea nudged Phoenix's arm to turn her around. Charlie, head still cradled on his arms, blinked at them silently.

"He was." Phoenix sighed. She moved back to Charlie and offered him a smile as she studied him. "Do you feel okay, bud? Are you tired?"

He nodded but said nothing.

"Did you check the church?" Lynnea asked.

"No."

"You can't go in the church," Charlie whispered.

"Why not?"

But he didn't respond. Phoenix wondered briefly if this was a dream. If she would wake up at any moment to live this day, the Halloween program, for real.

"I'll look." Lynnea ducked out of the room. Phoenix decided she should let Charlie's dad know they were running a bit late. She wasn't ready to sound the alarm that Anthony was missing, but she could tell Tom they hadn't left the church yet.

But mud on the hall floor drew her eye. She looked to her left, to the restrooms again, both still lighted after she had gone in to look for Anthony. Behind her she heard humming again, a mix of words both wrong and correct to "Aikendrum." She stole a quick peek into the kitchen to see that now it was Charlie humming. Unnerved, she bit her tongue before she could give the boy hell and tell him to be quiet. She might be frazzled, but it would pay to play it calm right now.

The women's room was empty still. No four-year-old boy standing on a toilet to hide in a stall. No crazy woman other than herself in the mirror. Phoenix flipped the light off and considered closing the door as she stepped back out. The thought of having to search in there again and having to open the door to darkness stopped her.

Water dripped in the men's room. She heard the tiny, repeated tink, tink, tink before she saw it. Anthony stood under the mirror drawing circles in the base of the sink. Phoenix noticed that his cheap, second-hand hiking boots were caked with mud.

He hummed again, but when he realized she was in the room, he gave her a lopsided smile and sang out loud about the woods. Still to the tune of "Aikendrum", but she hadn't taught any lyrics of the song about the woods.

"Anthony, where were you?"

"I went outside." He shrugged and turned his attention back to the sink. For a moment, Phoenix was afraid to look into the sink, afraid of what she would find. The worry of the dead animals out back weighed on her.

"Why? Anthony, you can't do that, kiddo. You scared me and Miss Lynnea."

"He said I should."

"Who said you should?" She took a deep breath and took the last step. Lungs frozen, she peered into the sink and sagged with relief when she saw only dirty drops of water there.

"The devy man."

## 4

Phoenix didn't flinch, but Anthony's singsong declaration that the devy man told him to go outside creeped her out. She swallowed hard, did a mental shiver, and propped her hands on her hips.

"The devy man, huh?" She had to dig deep to pull out the bubbly teacher voice, but she didn't want to play into Anthony's imagination. Not now. She was beat; it was time for all of them to go home.

"He's my friend." Anthony's solemn nod and doe eyes hit her in her own imagination. She gave him an exasperated smile and stepped toward him to herd him out of the bathroom.

"Did your brothers make that up? Is it a game?" she asked as she dropped her hands on his shoulders and steered him toward the door.

"They don't know about him," he argued, but he let Phoenix head him out of the bathroom.

"Lynnea, I found him!" she called as she walked Anthony into the kitchen. Charlie was still seated at the table, eyes on his folded hands. He appeared tired, but his nose was no longer bleeding, and he looked up when she and Anthony entered the room. Phoenix breathed a silent sigh of relief when he tracked their movements. The catatonic stare was unnerving. "Charlie, do you know where Miss Lynnea is?"

"No."

Well, at least Charlie answered her. Phoenix puffed up her cheeks and released her breath slowly. She needed to tell Lynnea that she'd found Anthony. But she had no intention of leaving either boy here alone while she searched for her. Instead, she pulled a chair out and urged Anthony to sit down.

"Are you guys hungry?"

She would just have to wait for Lynnea or Ross to come back inside. They would understand.

"No." Anthony beamed at her from his spot at the table. Anthony's family was big, and they weren't exactly neglectful of him. But Phoenix thought he always seemed starved for attention and love.

"Charlie?" She glanced at the other boy, but he barely shook his head in response. "What happens when you guys go to bed? Do you take a bath first? Does someone read you a story?"

She hopped up on the counter as Lynnea had just minutes before.

"Quentin and Daddy fight," Charlie announced. "And the kinda-mom reads to me."

Phoenix almost asked Charlie to repeat himself, but she realized she'd heard him right. The kinda-mom— apparently how he referred to his dad's girlfriends. Maybe some of them didn't last long enough for Charlie to even learn their names. The heel of her hand pressed to her chest to ease the stab of pain his words brought, Phoenix smacked her lips together and managed to make her mouth curve up.

"That's fun."

Even precocious and sometimes mean Charlie liked stories.

"Anthony, how about you?"

She glanced from Charlie to Anthony in time to see the boy shake his head. His brown eyes were glued to the table now, but he was frowning.

"I get scared," he whispered.

"At night?"

He raised his head to look at her, brown eyes wide with fear.

"Do you sleep with a nightlight?"

"It doesn't work," he mumbled.

Phoenix held her breath for a second. Dennis Hale couldn't pull himself together long enough to put a new lightbulb in his son's nightlight? She made a mental note to ask Dennis or April, Anthony's mom, about it. Maybe she would pick one up just to make sure the kid could sleep at night.

"And the tapping at the window scares me."

"Tapping at the—?"

"Phoenix?" Lynnea's voice called from the hall outside the kitchen. "Did you find—"

"Yes, I did." Phoenix nodded when Lynnea appeared in the doorway. "Didn't want to leave them alone to find you and Ross to tell you."

Lynnea nodded and waved her words away, but she watched Anthony, probably looking for injuries or bite marks or something out of the ordinary, just as Phoenix had done in the bathroom.

"Where was he?" Lynnea finally turned her attention to Phoenix.

"I found him in the bathroom." She jumped down from the counter and stood for a moment watching the boys. "His boots are caked with mud. He said he was outside."

"I went to see the devy man." Anthony looked at Lynnea, his wicked grin totally at odds with the four-year-old face and voice that had only seconds ago told Phoenix he gets scared at night.

"The devy man," Lynnea repeated. She peeked at Phoenix and shrugged. "Okay."

"Is Ross still out there?" Phoenix asked.

"Yeah, he's still looking for Anthony."

"I'll go tell him he's safe."

She didn't wait for Lynnea to argue with her. Rather, she moved quickly out of the room, down the short hall, and opened the door to go outside. Already chilled, the nip in the air made her shiver as she wandered around the gravel lot looking for Ross.

"Ross?" she called, and then she strained to hear his response or to hear him calling for Anthony. When she heard nothing, she stuffed her hands in the hip pockets of her corduroy pants and wandered out farther from the building. After a few steps, a putrid odor made her gag. The dead animals, she realized.

"Ross?" she yelled a little louder this time. She wasn't afraid of dead animals, but she wasn't crazy about the idea of seeing them or breathing in the stench, either. Ahead of her, she heard leaves crunching underfoot. "Ugh." She sighed and then drew a deep breath to steel herself. The church was surrounded on two sides by wooded property. Ross was probably out tracking through the woods looking for Anthony; he wouldn't hear her if he was even just a few steps into the trees.

Naturally, she would have to walk right past the dead animals to go in the direction of the noise she'd just heard. As she walked, the sounds from the woods grew louder; she would find Ross, wait for Dennis to get Anthony, and then take Charlie home. She most definitely planned to take a shower, but she was so tired now, she would skip the glass of wine.

"Ross?" she called again, but now she could taste the ripe odor back here by the woods. In her peripheral vision, she could see a small pile, but she commanded herself not to look. "Ross? We found him."

The crunching of leaves stopped suddenly. Phoenix stood for a moment, just past the dead animals, and held her breath. Eyes on the trees in front of her, she waited for Ross to appear. When he didn't, she opened her mouth to call to him again.

The hair on the back of her neck stood on end. She would swear there was someone, something, in the woods, looking back at her. Ridiculous, because it was dark enough in the far reaches of the parking lot where she stood. It was nearly black as pitch in the woods. She couldn't see a thing out here. If there was something in the woods looking at her, she would never know for certain.

Pressure in her bladder made her squirm a bit. Never mind Ross. She wasn't going into the woods alone. Not in the dark. Not that she was afraid there was really someone hiding in the trees, watching her. But the trees and the undergrowth were thick and difficult to navigate. In the darkness, it would be treacherous to attempt it. She might end up getting lost.

Still. She couldn't shake the feeling that something was watching her.

The pungent smell of death was making her nauseas. Ready to vomit, she started to turn away but stopped and froze halfway twisted around. Something red glowed in the trees, like two eyes looking back at her.

"Phoenix?"

She jumped and yelped when she felt someone touch her shoulder.

"Good grief, Ross." She sucked in a deep breath as she turned to find Ross at her side. "You scared me to death."

"Sorry." He shook his head. "What're you doing? You didn't find him?"

"We did. I was looking for you to tell you."

"Okay." He nodded. "What're you looking at?" He leaned her way to study the woods from her vantage point. She waited for a second, to see if he mentioned the red glow, but when he said nothing, she only shook her head.

"Just looking for you," she mumbled. She took one last long look for herself, but the glowing red lights were gone. Just her overactive imagination, she decided as she turned and fell into step beside Ross to head back to the church. She still felt exposed, as if someone was watching her. Easy to write it off as an overactive imagination with all the weird little things that had happened tonight.

But, on the other hand, she had felt this way all day, not just tonight since Ross had announced to her that

Charlie and Anthony were still at the church, since Anthony started talking about the devy man.

The low rumble of a truck engine drew her attention to the road out front. Dennis Hale's headlights swept the lot as he turned in and parked willy-nilly in front of the door. Okay for now, since there was no one else around. The trouble was Dennis tended to break the rules all the time. For instance, the one about not drinking and driving. Phoenix picked up her step to hurry inside. Lynnea would know to pay attention to Dennis' mindset and his sobriety, too, but Phoenix still needed to be inside to talk to him before releasing Anthony to him.

Ross pulled the door open for her. Just as her foot hit the small lip of the doorway, she heard a long, low mournful howl behind her. She hadn't imagined it; there was something in the woods out there. Some bigger animal, a predator, had been killing those animals, and just a few moments ago, it might have been sizing her up.

Did coyotes howl?

Lynnea and Dennis stood by the cubbies when she went inside. Dennis peeked at Phoenix over Lynnea's shoulder and offered her an apologetic smile.

"Sorry, Phoenix." He lifted a bony shoulder in a lazy shrug. "Workin' some odd hours. Jovi dropped him off. I must have fallen asleep as soon as she left."

Phoenix folded her arms over her chest as she moseyed up close to stand with him and Lynnea.

"Where's April tonight?"

She couldn't be obvious; she couldn't lean into him and sniff for the telltale scent of liquor. Then again, the smell of death and varying states of decay out back might have singed her nostrils. Dennis might smell like a distillery for all she knew. She glanced at Lynnea, relieved to see that she was casually propped at the end of the cubbies.

"She's in Jester with friends."

"Hmm." Phoenix nodded. "I know she'll be bummed that she missed the program. The kids did a great job tonight."

April Hale wouldn't be bummed for missing the program. Being in Jester with friends wasn't a good excuse for missing your youngest child's school activities. The jab was lost on Dennis, too, but Phoenix still felt a smidge better for having said it.

"I'll get Anthony." Lynnea stirred beside her. The look on her face when their eyes met told Phoenix that she had caught Phoenix's intended shame on April.

"How's he doing?" Dennis nodded in Lynnea's direction. Phoenix remembered that she was going to ask Dennis about the nightlight.

"He's doing well," she said simply. And he was. Anthony was developmentally on track, if not advanced. Phoenix just wished he had better hygienic habits. But, then, those were taught in the home, right? And Phoenix reinforced those good lessons when she could. She eyed Dennis quietly when he swung his head around to take in their surroundings. Not a big leap to see why Anthony looked and dressed as he did. "I think you might want to say something to the big kids, though. He's been talking about someone called the devy man."

Dennis gaped at her and shrugged. "No idea what that is."

"Well, whatever it is, it's almost Halloween, and he's four. I think it's scaring him."

"I'll talk to them."

"Also, Anthony said his nightlight is broken."

"Nah, it's fine."

"Really? He specifically said it doesn't work."

"It's on every night when he goes to bed."

"Okay, Anthony." Lynnea's voice hit that teacher note —the mix of excitement with exhaustion. "Here's Dad."

Lynnea helped Anthony put his jacket on. Phoenix eyed his bib overalls and the flannel shirt beneath. She still wasn't sure if it was a costume—was he a scarecrow, maybe?—or just a regular outfit—he wore the same items now and then—because April forgot about the Halloween activities today.

Phoenix walked Dennis and Anthony to the door and stood watch while Dennis buckled the boy into his car seat in the back seat of the truck cab. She nodded and returned Dennis' wave and then turned and ran smack into Lynnea.

"I didn't smell any alcohol."

"Neither did I." Phoenix shook her head. "Let's get Charlie and get out of here."

Lynnea collected Charlie from the kitchen and handed him his fleece jacket. A hand-me-down from Quentin, it fit him big and loose, dwarfing him. At least he looked warm. Phoenix gathered her phone and her purse. She flipped lights off as they all moved to the back of the building, one hand groping for her keys.

Ross stood at the back door. He offered them both a tired smile, said goodnight to Charlie, and pushed the door closed. Phoenix and Lynnea said goodnight, and Phoenix buckled Charlie into the car seat she had purchased a few years ago for just this kind of occasion.

As she settled into the driver's seat and locked her door, she glanced at Ross, who was locking the back door. Her eyes moved from Ross to the rearview mirror, where she saw Charlie resting with his head on the seat, eyes closed. He did look pale and tired. Maybe he *was* coming down with something.

She started the SUV and put the vehicle in drive. Creeping through the gravel, she looked again at the woods.

Why, if whatever had been watching her was an animal, did it get quiet and disappear only when Ross joined her in the parking lot?

## 5

Phoenix wanted to laugh at the unease she felt when she pulled into the gravel church lot the next day. After all, daylight had a way of chasing away the monsters and nightmares. Still, there was a residual creepiness about the night before that lingered. Tom Baker hadn't wanted to talk to her last night. Judging from the way he had shooed Charlie inside and up to his bedroom, Phoenix assumed the kinda-mom was keeping Tom's bed warm while he parented for a few more minutes.

Still, she had elbowed her way inside and stood in the kitchen for a few minutes to talk to Tom about Charlie's nosebleeds. Tom, dressed in a white undershirt and old, loose-fitting sweatpants, leaned on the counter at his back and listened to her concerns. He'd said he had noticed the nosebleeds, but he figured the air was dry, and it wasn't a big deal. Phoenix tried to press the matter. She asked if he had noticed how quiet, how lethargic Charlie had been lately. Tom said no, but again, Phoenix figured he was in a hurry to get rid of her and would say anything to get her out the door.

Once home, she had showered and dressed in flannel pajama pants and a long-sleeved thermal shirt. She had still felt cold, and she couldn't shake the feeling that someone was watching her. She skipped the wine, watched some TV just to decompress after the long day, and climbed into bed by midnight. She'd slept fitfully, though thankfully, there hadn't been any dreams about dead animals or rabid coyotes slinking around in the woods.

Now, inside the church, Phoenix made coffee. Lynnea would be in today and tomorrow only for a half day. Phoenix didn't always need the extra pair of hands, but she didn't want to be alone in the church after last night so she was happy Lynnea would arrive shortly. The light was on in the church office, and she had seen Pastor Tweedy's Prius parked out front, so when he wandered through the community room on the way to the men's room, she was prepared for him.

The guy was nice, too nice, probably. Phoenix thought he was a throwback to *Happy Days* or something, right down to his slicked back hair and sweater vests. They chatted some about the program the night before; Pastor Tweedy and his wife had been there for the performance, though they hadn't stayed for the social hour. They were the age of most of the preschool parents, but they didn't have children. At any rate, Phoenix wouldn't admit it, but his presence today was a comfort.

Lynnea arrived within the hour. She took the Halloween decorations down and tidied up the play areas and kitchen while Phoenix caught up on lesson planning and updating the kids' progress reports. With the radio on and pop music playing, the day passed without event, which suited Phoenix just fine. They heard through the grapevine that Carter's condition had been upgraded to stable, and after sharing their relief for Carter and his family, they discussed Charlie and his nosebleeds. Neither of them was thrilled that Tom hadn't taken Phoenix's concern seriously, but they couldn't force him to worry about it, either.

They left before full dark claimed the skies, but Phoenix still eyed the back of the lot and the woods suspiciously as she left. Ross had taken care of the dead animal carcasses, but she had no idea what exactly that meant. With a shudder of revulsion, she decided as long as the mess was gone, she didn't want to know.

Since she skipped the wine the night before, she had a glass with her frozen pizza. The vintage made up for the less than delicious meal. With her lights turned down low, she curled up in the corner of her couch to binge watch her favorite TV drama. Forgetting how badly the night before at the church had spooked her, she changed the channel after a few hours and got involved in a slasher film.

She liked a good scary movie now and then, and as the movie played on her TV, she laughed at herself for getting spooked the night before. True, the night had been a little unnerving—especially when Anthony vanished for a few minutes—but she had let Anthony's wild, childish imagination influence her own. She would attribute some of that to the time of year and some to the fact that she was overly exhausted.

When she got sleepy there on the couch, she gave in

and dozed off. That was one of the nice things about living alone. If she fell asleep watching TV and woke up at three in the morning, it didn't matter. She wouldn't wake anyone else when she got up and turned the lights and TV off to go to bed.

A loud, incessant ringing woke her. Deeply asleep, she tried to turn over and only managed to smoosh her face into the sofa cushions. The ringing continued. Phoenix finally threw off the blanket she'd covered herself with and sat up.

Her phone rang and vibrated on the coffee table in front of her. She squinted at the TV; the light hurt her eyes. With a yawn, she swiped her hand over her face and then picked up her phone. It was just after midnight. The number on her screen belonged to April Hale.

A surge of energy swept through her. Her fingers tingled with nerves as she pressed the home button to answer the call.

"April?"

"Phoenix."

Definitely April, though she sounded distracted and a little bit frazzled.

"Yeah, April, it's me. What's wrong?" She stood, already looking around for her shoes. Still dressed, she ducked into the bathroom and looked in the mirror.

"It's Anthony." April added something, but it sounded like she was mumbling, maybe talking to someone else.

"What about Anthony? What can I do?"

"He's missing, Phoenix."

This time, the rush of fear and energy made her cold.

"What do you mean he's missing?"

"He's missing!"

Phoenix flinched at April's half sob and half shout.

"Okay. I'm on my way."

"Come to the house."

Phoenix ended the call. She pushed her hair back from her face, skipped any primping, and hurried out to the living area again. Her shoes were in front of the couch, and she danced, hopping from foot to foot, as she put them on. Finally, she shrugged her jacket on, turned the TV off, and grabbed her keys.

She wondered about calling Lynnea, but as she backed her SUV out of the driveway, she decided against it. Maybe in the morning. Lynnea had a family; she didn't want to disturb them now when she had nothing to tell her other than that Anthony was missing.

The Hales' house on Bauer was average for the street and surrounding homes. Tonight, it appeared that every light in the house was on, and the golden light cast from all the windows lit up the small, patchwork yards surrounding them. Still, darkness hovered at the periphery, and Phoenix's shoulders twitched with an irrational fear as she climbed from her car and looked around. The yard, such as it was, was crawling with people: neighbors, surely, as well as friends and family. Being a rural community, there was no local police presence. Ivy, as well as other small towns in the county, fell under state police and the sheriff's jurisdiction.

Phoenix sighed with relief when she saw the sheriff's car parked crossways at the end of the short drive, which consisted only of two strips of dead grass where tire ruts had worn it away over time. In the next breath, her stomach seized and cramped with nerves. If Sheriff

Baxter was here, Anthony's disappearance this time seemed much more real.

"Phoenix!" Jovi spotted her and ran across the yard as she approached the small front porch. The front door stood open, but it wasn't a warm welcome. The abandoned doorway leading into the front room—the lamplight almost dingy up close—spoke more to April and Dennis' desperation.

"What's going on?" Phoenix settled her hands on the girl's upper arms to hold her still long enough to get the story.

Jovi stared back at Phoenix, frightened eyes wide and unblinking. Even in the semi-shadows, just outside the light of the house, Phoenix could make out the dried tears on Jovi's face.

"Mom—" Jovi started and stopped to sob and then sniffle and start again. "Mom came downstairs to check on Dad. She woke him up from the recliner, and they were going upstairs to bed. She..." Again, Jovi stopped talking. Phoenix wanted to shake her, to make her spill the details quicker, so she could join the search. But she only took a deep breath and waited for Jovi to get a hold of herself. Of all of the five Hale children, Jovi struck Phoenix as the most responsible and the closest to Anthony, the baby of the family.

"And then what, Jovi?" Phoenix spoke softly, wanting to comfort the girl, as well as coax her into sharing the rest of the story.

"She always checks on us as she goes to bed. Like. Every time she gets up to get a drink or go to the bathroom or whatever, she peeks in to check on us. I've seen her do it a hundred times when I'm not sleeping yet." Jovi hiccupped and swiped at her eyes. "When she checked on Anthony, he was gone."

"Gone."

Jovi nodded, eyes even wider than before.

"What time was this?"

Phoenix decided she should probably be talking to April or Dennis, though she wasn't sure either of them would be any more reliable or coherent than Jovi, Dennis probably less so. Maybe she should scout out the sheriff and see what he had to say about the situation.

"Like...an hour ago." Jovi swiped at her nose with her hand and looked over her shoulder at the house. "His bed was...perfect. Like the comforter and sheet turned back, like in a hotel room or something. The way you see in movies, in fancy hotels."

Phoenix nodded.

"It didn't look like he'd even been in the bed, Mom said, but she tucked him in when it was his bedtime."

"What time does Anthony go to bed?" Phoenix asked her.

"Sometimes eight. Eight-thirty."

Phoenix wondered exactly what time Anthony had gone outside last night at the church. She needed to tell someone about the incident. Once she had found Anthony last night, unharmed, and he told her he had gone outside for a minute, she folded the incident up and put it away. He was a little boy who liked to play outside, and he'd slipped out into the dark for a few minutes. Maybe the timing didn't make a bit of difference, but in light of what was going on right now, Phoenix knew any bit of information she could offer might help.

"Where's your mom?"

"His window was open, Phoenix," Jovi whispered.

A late October night—technically Halloween, Phoenix realized, since it was after midnight— brought its own innate chills. The air was damp, and the wind a little bit brisk, but it was Jovi's words and her tone that made Phoenix shudder.

"His window—?" Phoenix tipped her head and eyed Jovi curiously. When Jovi only nodded, Phoenix lifted her gaze to peer at the house over the girl's shoulder. "Like, when your mom put him to bed, the window was open? Because it was stuffy in his room?"

"No!" Jovi sounded exasperated now. "No, like when Mom saw that he was gone, his window was open."

Phoenix thought back to last night when Anthony had told her about his broken nightlight—the one Dennis had assured her worked just fine. Anthony had also said the tapping on the window scared him. Tapping on a window after dark would scare anyone, most definitely a four-year-old, but Phoenix remembered now she hadn't had a chance to question him about it because Lynnea had come inside then, unaware that Phoenix had found him.

Now she wondered how in the hell anyone could have tapped on Anthony's window. All the bedrooms in the Hale house were on the second floor.

"Okay." She nodded, hoped she sounded calm, responsible, even though she desperately wished she weren't an adult right now, and she was grateful this was over her head and the sheriff was handling it. But she still had to find the sheriff, find April and Dennis, and tell them that Anthony had slipped away from her for all of five or ten minutes the night before. It sounded pretty damning now, certainly made her feel like she was somehow responsible for his disappearance tonight. "I need to talk to your parents. The sheriff. Someone in charge."

Jovi wiped her eyes and turned toward the house to lead Phoenix inside. She had been there on home visits so often through the past year and a half that the worn brown microfiber sofa and the broken cuckoo clock were as familiar to her as the things in her own home. Though two stories, the house was small. The rooms were all crammed into the same spaces leaving Phoenix feeling claustrophobic, like half the house was piled on top of her, pinning her down and stealing her breath.

She heard conversation in the tiny dining area, one voice most definitely belonging to April Hale. The smell of grease lingered in the air, but Phoenix also smelled freshly brewed coffee. They were digging in for a long night of searching. Phoenix swallowed down a mouthful of bile as she stepped into the room and April and Deputy Caroline Webb turned their attention to her.

"Any ideas?" she asked by way of greeting. April looked old and tired on a good day; Phoenix supposed having five kids could do that to you. Tonight, she looked like hell. Her hair hung in long, flat curls, and the remains of yesterday's mascara was smudged around her eyes and over her face. She must have grabbed the closest clothing she could find when she realized Anthony was gone. Phoenix recognized the sweater she wore as one she favored when she was out with friends, but on her legs, she wore what appeared to be khakis that most likely belonged to Dennis.

"No one heard anything. No neighbors saw anything. He's just gone."

Without asking, April poured coffee for Phoenix and

shoved it at her. Phoenix didn't want it, but she took it and lowered herself to sit at the table across from the deputy. Webb was older. Her stocky build and broad shoulders lent her a kickass aura, and her gray hair pulled back in a crisp, neat ponytail spoke of her no-nonsense demeanor. Phoenix liked her; she was glad she was here with April.

"Sheriff's organizing a search," Webb told Phoenix. "Marking off grids and making search groups."

Phoenix nodded. "Okay. Where is he? I wanna help."

"He'll holler when they're ready," Webb assured her. "We're gonna go about this systematically. Make sure we're covering as much ground as possible, and we need to make sure we don't go crashing around and destroying any evidence."

"Evidence?" The word crawled up and out of Phoenix's mouth before she could stop it. April gagged and then sobbed and covered her eyes.

"Most likely, Anthony wandered off."

"Wandered off?" April repeated. She dropped her hands to her sides and folded herself into a chair at the table. "None of my kids has ever wandered off, especially not in the dark."

"He might have been sleepwalking," Webb suggested.

"I already told you he's never done that before."

"But it doesn't mean he didn't do it tonight."

"How do you explain the open window?" Phoenix asked Deputy Webb.

The woman sighed and shrugged. "There's a downspout that runs from the roof to the foundation about a foot to the left of his window."

"And you think a four-year-old is going to climb out

his window in the dark and shimmy down the spout? What? Like he wanted to be the itsy-bitsy spider?"

Phoenix recognized the frustration in April's ragged voice.

"Probably not." Webb flinched. She reached over the table to cover April's hand with her own. "We'll find him."

"Anthony's afraid of the dark."

Phoenix looked at April quickly. "Does he sleep with a nightlight?"

"Yeah."

"Was it on? When you checked in his room earlier?"

"Why do you ask?" Webb directed the question to Phoenix.

"I—" April frowned. "I wanna say yes. Of course, it was. But I don't really know. I turned it on earlier when I put him in bed."

"He told me last night that it's broken."

April shook her head. "No. I turn it on every night."

Phoenix sighed. Her head pounded with the bits of information that she couldn't piece together to make sense.

"Have you ever heard him talk about the devy man?"

April nodded, but she stared at Phoenix with impatience, like Phoenix was wasting her time.

"Yeah. The kids play some kind of tag game outside. In the back. The devy man is it."

"Okay." Phoenix finally remembered the coffee April had shoved at her and took a small drink. "Last night, after the Halloween program—"

"That was last night?" April sounded shocked.

"Well, Wednesday night." Phoenix made a show of

pulling her phone from her back pocket and eyeing the screen. "It's technically Friday now."

"I forgot." April groaned out loud and clapped her hands over her ears. "Dammit. I forgot all about it."

"Jovi dropped Anthony off," Phoenix told her. "But she had a date. And Dennis was late picking him up."

April answered with a slight nod.

"I had Charlie Baker there late, too. The boys were in the big room at the table. Anthony was drawing."

A burst of voices sounded from outside and drew their attention to the window over the kitchen sink. Phoenix wondered what the holdup was; shouldn't they be out there now searching for Anthony? It was entirely possible he had simply wandered off and gotten lost in the woods.

Possible, too, that whatever animal had sized Phoenix up the other night outside the church had attacked the little boy. They needed to find him now.

"Charlie had a nosebleed, so I took him to the kitchen to clean him—"

"Wait." April shook her head. "What? A nosebleed?"

"Yeah. I took him—"

"Like a gushing nosebleed? Messy?"

"No. Not at first. Just a drop of blood."

"That almost looked black?"

"Mm-hmm." Phoenix nodded. "Why?"

"Because Aiden had one yesterday."

Phoenix rubbed her eyes and then rested her chin on her hand. Eight-year-old Aiden was a lot like Anthony. Phoenix had never taught him, but he was sweet to her and always excited to see her.

"And Anthony had one tonight—well, before I put him in bed."

"That's weird." Phoenix sighed and pressed her fingers to her forehead between her eyebrows. Charlie. Tyler Camden. Aiden Hale. Anthony. Throw in the recent accidents—that was a lot of blood in Ivy.

"What happened? When you were in the kitchen with Charlie?" Deputy Webb urged Phoenix to go on.

"Um." She shook her head and shrugged. "I cleaned him up. I could see Anthony through the big window in the wall. Lynnea came inside to tell me about that crash on the highway, and then Charlie did have a nosebleed. Like gushing bright red that time, so I was cleaning him up again. Lynnea went to call Tom and you." Here, she nodded at April. "I looked up again, and Anthony was gone."

"I'm sorry?" Webb tipped her head. April watched her through slitted eyes; Phoenix's face burned under April's righteous anger.

"He was gone. We panicked—"

"And you didn't think to tell Dennis that? When he picked him up?"

"No." Phoenix sighed and shrugged again. "No. Like I said, we panicked. Lynnea went outside to look for him. Ross was out there, so he started looking. I searched the church. On my second round, I found him in the men's room."

"And?" Webb shook her head.

"And nothing. He was fine. There was fresh mud caked on his boots. He was playing in the sink. Kind of patting his hands in dirty water. But that's it. He was out of sight for, like, five—seven minutes, maybe."

April sniffled and wiped at her eyes.

"When it was happening, when we were all scrambling

to find him, it felt like it lasted forever. But then there he was, and he was fine. He told me the devy man had told him to go outside."

April rolled her eyes.

"Great. So, my older kids have scared the bejesus out of him with some creature they made up and who's always *it* when they play tag, and that made up creature talked my baby into going outside. I supposed that's what happened here?"

She shot that last question at Deputy Webb.

"Let's not jump to conclusions," Webb said calmly.

"Can Anthony open his own window?"

"I suppose he could, but I've never seen him do it. And it was open wide." April looked toward the kitchen window again.

"When I found him in the bathroom, I took him back to the kitchen with me. So, I asked him and Charlie both what their bedtime routine is. That's when Anthony told me his nightlight is broken." Phoenix rubbed her own eyes. Being awake at this late hour made them gritty, and the nap she'd grabbed on the couch was a poor substitute for a good eight hours of sleep.

"It's not broken," April insisted.

Phoenix nodded quickly to calm April down. "He also said that the tapping on his window scares him."

"Tapping on his window?" Webb frowned.

"Yeah. I didn't get a chance to question him, because then Lynnea came inside to see if I had found him. After that, things went fast. I went out to tell Ross everything was okay; Lynnea stayed with Anthony and Charlie. That's when Dennis came to get Anthony."

"I don't think anyone can climb that downspout up to a window," April argued. "Not an adult."

"Probably not," Phoenix agreed. Frankly, she thought the whole house might shift and fold in on itself if someone tried to climb anything about it, especially an adult-sized body.

"We'll be looking for footprints around the house," Webb assured them both. "But I'll have the sheriff come in to take your statement."

Phoenix wanted to argue. It wasn't much of a statement, was it? Just odd things a little boy had said.

"April, does Anthony talk about school much?""

"All the time." April's smile was small and forlorn. "He likes the water table."

Phoenix grinned. "That's our science area. Doesn't surprise me."

"He likes dirt. He's always digging out back. Dennis and I joke that he'll be an excavator when he's older. He likes the songs, too." April stood up and fetched the coffee pot from the burner to top off Webb's and her cups. She glanced at Phoenix's barely touched cup and then returned the pot to the coffee maker. "He makes me nuts with that. He's always singing. And he gets one song stuck in his head and hums it for weeks at a time."

Phoenix nodded and offered April a smile.

"Lately, it's that one about Odell Dunn."

"What one about Odell Dunn?"

"You know. The man who lived in the woods."

Phoenix shook her head. "No. I taught them a song called 'Aikendrum.' He lived in the moon."

## 6

A pril stared at Phoenix for a moment, finally stirring and shrugging away the information.

"Well, Anthony sings it as Odell Dunn."

"How does Anthony know anything about Odell Dunn?" Webb gulped her coffee, put the cup down with a bit too much force, and turned a puzzled frown to April.

"Wait. Who's Odell Dunn?"

"He was an old man who lived on County Road 669E," Webb told Phoenix. "Lived alone. Kept mostly to himself."

"He was creepy," April told Phoenix. "The way he watched people. He would stand in front of Dottie's Market and just stare at women as they went in and out. Rumor has it he sold drugs and had a stockpile of weapons in his house."

"Rumors are a waste of time, April," Webb scolded her. "The man was odd, but he was mostly harmless."

Phoenix opened her mouth to ask why they were wasting time arguing about a man named Odell Dunn, but April snorted at Deputy Webb.

"Harmless? Didn't he do time for assault?"

Webb flinched. "He did. Yes. Okay, not harmless. But he didn't have a stockpile of weapons. And while he appeared to use drugs, it was never proven that he was a dealer."

"And what happened to him?" Phoenix sipped her coffee.

"Disappeared. I think he left town. The bank wanted to foreclose on his shack, but it wasn't worth a dime. Neither was the land it was built on. Backs up to Sapphire Creek. Big storm about twenty years back tore through and took down a bunch of trees. One fell on the back side of the house. Dunn didn't do anything to clean it up."

"So, you think he skipped town? To get out of clean up and debt and whatever else he had going on?"

Webb shrugged now.

"Dunn was a nasty man," April told Phoenix. "Kids hate him, mostly because they're afraid of him. You know how kids are. If he were a woman, he would be the old, hag witch kids whisper about. His house is haunted. If he catches you around his property, he'll dismember you and eat you."

"Dismember you?" Phoenix shivered and squeezed her eyes closed. "God, when I was a kid, the boogie man was more like the witch in *Hansel and Gretel* than Jeffrey Dahmer."

April clapped her hand over her mouth and closed her eyes. Phoenix looked away when she noticed tears sliding over April's cheeks and hand.

"We need to find Anthony."

"April, he probably just wondered off. The way he did after the program."

April shook her head and mumbled something into her hand.

"He likes science. He likes to be outside. You said yourself he likes to dig."

All true, Phoenix reminded herself. Though, on the other hand, if he was afraid of the dark, she didn't believe he had gotten out of bed, climbed out his window, and wandered around outside to play in the woods.

"Do you remember the song he was singing?" Phoenix asked April.

"Something about Odell." April swiped at her nose and cleared her throat.

"But do you remember any of the words?"

"Um." April licked her lips. "There was a man who lived in the woods, in the woods, in the woods. There was a man who lived in the woods, and his name was Odell Dunn."

Phoenix sighed. So similar to "Aikendrum" that she had to assume the older kids had made up different lyrics about Odell Dunn to scare the little kids.

"And he ate…upon…" April tipped her head. "He ate upon a cradle? No. Maybe a table? And his name was Odell Dunn."

Deputy Webb's radio spilled some nonsense codes; the disembodied voice in the kitchen tracing a chill up Phoenix's spine.

"Where are the rest of the kids?" Phoenix asked April.

"With my sister-in-law. At her house."

Webb gripped the radio on her shoulder with her fingers and spoke into it as she stood. Phoenix and April watched her head out of the house through the back door.

"And his hair was made of black weeds." April pushed

her balled fists into her eye sockets, obviously still trying to remember the song Anthony had been singing. "And his eyes were made of red coals...he makes your nose bleed..."

Phoenix dragged her fingers back through her hair and shook her head. The lyrics were obviously supposed to frighten little kids, though they were still similar enough to fit the syllabic pattern of "Aikendrum."

"He'll get your head. He'll steal your brain. He'll roast your body on Samhain. He'll suck your blood and drain you dry. He'll drink your terror when you cry. He'll cast your soul to hell to brand, and you'll belong to the devy man."

Phoenix tore her eyes away from the back door. What was taking so long with the search?

"Wait." She shook her head. That last bit that April had recited more as a chant was new to her. She'd never heard anything like it. And she wasn't sure there was a song she'd taught her preschoolers to sing that followed the same rhyming pattern.

"Anthony sang that? The thing about the devy man?"

"All the time." April nodded.

"I don't know what that is." Phoenix shook her head.

"The older kids probably taught it to him."

Phoenix took a deep breath. Nerves ready to explode, she pushed her coffee cup aside.

"April, do you know where Odell Dunn's house is?"

"It's a shack, Phoenix," April told her. "And it's probably infested with rats. And snakes. The guy disappeared years ago."

Phoenix couldn't explain it. Her worry about the devy man. The way Anthony said the words in a singsong voice. Not terribly different than the way kids sang about the boogie man when she was a kid.

She didn't want to say that Charlie and Anthony had both referred to the devy man the other night. Because she would sound crazy. And yet, nothing about any of this made any sense, which Phoenix supposed was another way of saying it was all crazy.

"Do you know where it is?"

April nodded, but she lunged over the table to grab Phoenix's hand when she stood.

"You can't go there alone."

"You stay here. Call me if you hear something. When you find him."

"Phoenix, you can't just go to that house by yourself!"

"I'll call Lynnea." She lied to put April's mind at ease. Honestly, she didn't want to go to Odell Dunn's house by herself. Definitely not in the middle of the night. On Halloween. But she still didn't want to worry Lynnea. Not yet. And she couldn't drag anyone here away from the search for Anthony.

"I'll go with you," April announced as she stood up.

"You can't go with me. You need to be here."

"I need to find my son!" April snapped. "The Dunn house is as good a place as any to look."

"Is it far from here?"

"It's not a long drive, but it's a long way for a four-year-old to wander on his own."

"Let's go," Phoenix said with a nod.

April snatched up her own cell phone and tapped the screen as she followed Phoenix out the front door. The sheriff and the searchers were gathered now in the front yard. For a moment, Phoenix pictured each of them holding a flaming torch and was reminded of the days of lynch mobs and witch hunts.

"Move slowly. Look up. Watch the ground in the woods. Listen. Mark your trails. One time through, and then we wait for daybreak. I've contacted the state police, and they're sending a chopper. With night vision, they can see a lot more than we can."

Searching the woods this late at night would be extremely difficult. Phoenix was relieved to hear that the state police were sending a chopper. Thankfully, there were no cornfields close enough to the Hale home to worry about. There was no way four-year-old Anthony could possibly have wandered fifteen miles down the road and out of town to the Hoover farm.

When the sheriff finished speaking, the group broke up and smaller groups splintered in all directions. Dennis Hale approached April with a look of determination.

"We'll find him."

Phoenix lifted her eyes to look at the house again, tracking a downspout near the front window. Anthony's room was in the back of the house. If anyone had been sneaking around his window—and Phoenix *didn't* think it was possible—no one would have seen a thing.

"Phoenix and I are going to drive around and look."

Dennis glanced at Phoenix as if just realizing that she was there.

"Thank you." He nodded at her. She wished she had something encouraging to say, but her mind was blank. Dennis leaned in to drop a perfunctory kiss on April's cheek. "Keep your phone on."

April nodded silently and then followed Phoenix to her SUV.

"Which way do I go?" Phoenix asked when she started the engine.

"Do you think we should look anywhere else?"

"Where?" Phoenix threw the SUV into gear, clicked her seatbelt, and shot out of the spot in front of the yard.

"I don't know. Um." April was a frenzy of movement for a moment, pushing her hair from her face and rubbing her eyes. "Okay, you just drive, and I'll watch the roads. In case he's wandering around."

Phoenix nodded.

"Turn around up here and go back the other way," April directed her.

With Phoenix's nerves stretched to the limit, the soft music from the radio annoyed her. She clicked the power knob off and swung her little SUV in a wide arc at the open intersection at the end of the block. Though she wanted to step on it, to get to Odell Dunn's house as soon as possible, she crept along the street, and she and April both hunched forward as if they would be able to see better if they were closer to the windshield.

"That song," Phoenix started. "Was Anthony the only one to sing it?"

Hadn't she heard Charlie humming it in the church kitchen the other night? He'd definitely been humming the tune, but had he sung any actual words?

"About the man in the woods?" April asked, her head turned to her window. "No. All the kids sing it. All the time. Except Jovi. All I hear out of Jovi is Lizzo."

Phoenix wasn't sure what it meant, that all the kids sang the song about the man in the woods. But it was curious to her that Odell Dunn had supposedly vanished. Years ago. What if he hadn't?

"Even if Anthony wandered outside, he wouldn't just go to Odell Dunn's shack," April announced. Phoenix doubted that he would, too. She'd been teaching in this community for several years, and the name didn't ring a bell for her. How in the world would a four-year-old child know that name outside of a silly rhyming song older kids made up to scare him?

Unless he had been taken. What if Odell Dunn was back and no one realized it? If his place was such a nightmare, she doubted anyone ever went there on purpose. Then again, why in the world would some random old man decide to kidnap Anthony Hale?

What if it wasn't Odell Dunn, but *someone else* had taken him? She couldn't share her worries with April, though. Not yet.

"You're right," she said quietly, hoping to keep April calm. Beside her in the front of the car, April relaxed slightly. Phoenix turned her attention back to the streets again looking not just for Anthony, but for anything out of place.

Someone taking Anthony didn't seem right, either. Even a random someone. Because there was something weird going on in Ivy. The nosebleeds. Lynnea had reminded her the other night it wasn't just Charlie who had had the nosebleeds lately. And maybe they had nothing to do with anything, but the two major motor vehicle accidents that had happened recently bothered her, too. Stuff like that happened, happened all the time. But before the four-wheeler accident, it had been nearly two years since anyone had been injured, and that was Bob Corman, a sixty-three-year-old farmer whose tractor was hit by a car on the main road in town.

The fact that all the blood spilled lately in Ivy was young blood bothered Phoenix now that she thought about it.

"You think someone took him." April's flat tone pricked Phoenix's guilt. She sucked in a quick breath.

"No. Actually, I think the simplest solution is that he's sleepwalking."

"What about the window?"

"I don't know, April." Phoenix reached over to pat her friend's leg. "I don't know, but the only thing that makes any sense is that Anthony wandered off alone. And if he's that afraid of the dark, I think it makes sense to assume he was sleepwalking."

"He could get hurt in the woods." April shivered.

"He could, but we'll find him. If he's in the woods, the chopper will find him."

"When I was a kid back home, probably about four-teen, there was a little girl who wandered off and got lost in a cornfield." April flopped back in her seat as if she were suddenly exhausted. "Turn left up here."

Phoenix slowed the SUV and made a left where April indicated. They were only a few blocks from the Hale home, but it was too far away for Anthony to have come alone. If he had, Phoenix figured they would have seen him, maybe curled up by a tree, sleeping or lost and scared.

Still. Now that she'd set out to do this, to see Odell Dunn's home, she had to see it through. In all her years of teaching, she'd never been rattled by anything she heard students say or do. But the boys' humming the other night, Anthony's rendition of "Aikendrum" with the lyrics all wrong, and Anthony's disappearance from the church had gotten under her skin. It was ridiculous to think Odell Dunn had anything to do with Anthony's disappearance, but she would just feel better once she saw for herself that the house had been abandoned, and the man was still gone and posed no danger to any children in Ivy.

Phoenix drove the few blocks out of town and deeper into the sticks. In the absence of streetlights, the night was black as pitch, and rather than feel better, her unease grew bigger and harder in the pit of her belly.

"Is that it?" she asked April when her headlights swept over an old trailer. Weeds grew so high around it she almost missed it, but for the ancient Dodge Caravan parked in what she supposed was a yard. A stake in the ground and a chain leash suggested at one time whoever lived here had a dog, but Phoenix couldn't imagine anyone had been here in years. All four of the tires on the Caravan were flat, and the back window was bashed in, and even the cardboard repair job was ripped and curling inward with the damp weather.

"No."

Phoenix bit her tongue before she could speak. She was glad now that she hadn't come alone, but she felt guilty for dragging April away from the search for her son on what was probably, *hopefully*, a wild goose chase.

An opossum ran in front of the SUV, startling her enough that she cut loose with a sharp scream as she slammed on the brakes. The animal's eyes glowed in her headlights as it slinked on across the road.

"I hate Halloween," April mumbled.

"I thought I loved it," Phoenix said quietly. "Not so much this year."

She sucked in a deep breath and eased her foot off the

brake. They passed two more trailers in silence, one of them decked out with purple lights and some fancy, hi-tech Halloween decorations that probably cost more than the whole block of trailers and houses.

"Ever play with a Ouija board?"

In the dim light of the dashboard in the SUV, Phoenix felt April watching her.

"Nope." She shook her head. "I drew the line at *Light as a Feather, Stiff as a Board* when I was about thirteen." Phoenix glanced at April with a grin.

"My best friend had one," April told her. "She found it in her attic."

"And you tried it?"

April nodded.

"Anything ever happen?"

"The planchette moved, but I always assumed it was her doing it."

"That's just creepy," Phoenix mumbled. "I'll watch scary movies, but that's about it. I don't even like haunted houses."

"Oh, come on!" April laughed. "They're harmless."

"Maybe." Phoenix shrugged.

"That's it up there." April pointed at a small wooden shack, overgrown with weeds and plants crawling over the exterior walls.

"Eew." Phoenix flinched.

"Exactly."

She pulled the SUV to a stop across the dead county road, as if getting too close was dangerous.

"What're you doing?" April asked when she unclicked her seatbelt.

"Going to the door."

"Are you nuts?"

"April, he's just a man." Phoenix sounded far braver than she felt. Her heart hammered so hard; her chest hurt. But it was true. No one even knew if he was around now, and even if he was, Odell Dunn was just a man. Maybe he was shifty. Possibly dangerous, but Phoenix was prepared to find out. Just to knock on his door and see if he answered. To ask if he had seen Anthony Hale.

"I should have brought Dennis' gun." April clicked her seatbelt loose and opened her door.

"You don't have to go up there with me," Phoenix told her. She was glad April hadn't brought Dennis' gun. The last thing they needed was a frightened, stressed mother firing a gun in the dark. No matter if Odell had done time for assault or not, Phoenix didn't intend to shoot or harm the man.

"Don't be stupid," April argued.

Phoenix stepped out into silence. Only the trees whispered in a slight wind. No TV sounds this far out of town. No traffic. The quiet was natural, but for Phoenix, it felt anything, but.

"Ready?" she asked with a glance at April. The woman nodded without speaking, and together they crossed County Road 669E.

As they neared the house, Phoenix noticed the windows were boarded over. Had Odell done that before disappearing? Or had someone else come in and done that after he vanished? And why? If the man was truly gone, couldn't the county bulldoze the shack and be done with it?

"Does he have any family?"

"Not around here."

Phoenix nodded. Worried more about rodents and snakes than Odell himself, she tapped the flashlight app on her phone and eyed the uneven ground as they made their way to the front stoop. The tiny chunk of cement was cracked in half, one side completely crumbled away. Not enough room for both of them to stand at the door. Phoenix stepped forward and raised her fist to knock.

The sound shattered the quiet and made her jump.

While they waited, Phoenix tipped her head back and looked up. Through the bare branches overhead, she saw the moon and a few stars. A dormer window, though the house was small enough, she assumed it was part of a small attic rather than a second story. It, too, was boarded up. From where she stood, Phoenix noticed the wood was rotting, which suggested the windows had been boarded up for a long time.

Maybe Odell had done it himself.

Why?

Did he have something to hide?

She knocked again, but when no one answered, she twisted the doorknob.

"What are you doing?" April gasped as Phoenix pushed gently and the door opened with a loud squeak.

## 7

"Why are the windows boarded up?" Phoenix asked her.

"Maybe to keep animals out? Or kids?"

Probably, April was right. But if they had been boarded up that long, if Odell Dunn had done it before he disappeared, maybe he had something to hide. Phoenix didn't say that out loud, though, because again, it sounded crazy.

Odds were, the sheriff and the search teams had already found Anthony.

Then again, neither April's or her cell phone had buzzed with a call or text. So, while they were here, why not just do a quick peek inside?

"You're going inside?" April whispered. "Do you really think Anthony's in here?"

Phoenix was grateful April followed her inside, but she didn't say so. Instead, she shined the flashlight on her phone around the dark living area. The furniture was old and dirty, and cobwebs hung from the ceilings and light fixtures, but that was to be expected. The house smelled musty and old. Phoenix would guess no one had been here in quite a while.

She tiptoed through the living area and into a short hallway.

"Eww." She shivered when she shined her light into the bathroom. It smelled of mildew and urine, as if it hadn't ever been properly cleaned.

"Gross," April agreed.

Past the bathroom, she found a tiny bedroom, big enough to house a twin bed and a stark, old chest of drawers. Phoenix started forward, curious about the candle on the chest. Black. Burned down a bit, the wick blackened. Suddenly feeling that same sense of being watched, of exposure, she shivered and stepped back to leave the room.

"Phoenix," April whispered. She jumped when April snatched at her hand to turn her around. Hanging on the wall over the bed was an upside-down crucifix. Red letters spray painted on the wall around the crucifix drew her attention away from the blasphemously placed religious icon.

"What's it say?" Her voice was gruff.

"The Devy Man."

"Wow." Phoenix stepped closer to the wall and lifted her phone to see better. The paint had faded, leaving her to wonder how long it had been there. She considered taking the crucifix down, but she was afraid to touch it.

Rather, she moved her phone and eyed the simple iron bed frame and the faded denim blue quilt. The bed was made, but the pillowcase was filthy with what appeared to be dirt and blood and hair.

"Let's get out of here." She tugged gently at April's hand and led her back through the small hall. This time, she went the opposite way and found herself in the kitchen. A Pabst Blue Ribbon can lay on its side on a small red and white checkered table, stained with old food and rings from glasses. On the counter, an empty Jim Beam bottle sat next to an open book.

"Phoenix." April squeezed her hand.

Phoenix hung onto April, but she moved across the kitchen to look at the book. Again, she was afraid to touch it, so she only leaned closer to try and read a word or line. Cold dread rippled through her when she saw the words *black magic*.

April tugged at her hand, so she swung around to see what she wanted. On the wall above the red and white checked table, there were more spray-painted words.

*He'll cast your soul to hell to brand, and you'll belong to the devy man.*

"Someone's been in here," Phoenix whispered. Probably kids. Probably if they looked harder, they would find drug paraphernalia. Maybe porn. If they stuck around long enough, they might even get to meet the kids who were either squatting in Odell Dunn's shack or using it as a gathering place for getting high or orgies or maybe both.

And maybe playing at black magic.

Although, now and then there were stories in the news about satanic cults being busted for animal sacrifices, so Phoenix supposed it was possible whoever was sneaking in and out of Odell Dunn's shack might be adults who got off on weird stuff that she wanted no part of.

"Let's go." She pulled April toward the back door.

"Do you think it's just kids?" April asked her. Phoenix tried the door, but her hand slipped on the knob. She wiped it on the butt of her jeans and tried again. The knob didn't twist an inch. Phoenix gasped softly when she realized it was locked.

From the outside.

"Yep, probably." She tried to tiptoe and hurry at the same time back down the hall. Right now, her heart was in her throat, and she wasn't sure about anything. But probably, it was just harmless kids doing stupid things that would end up getting them in trouble. "That door was locked."

"From the outside?" April shrieked.

"Mm-hmm." Phoenix kept moving. "It's okay. We'll just go back out the way we came in. We'll get in the car and check in with Dennis, okay?"

"Yeah, okay. Good idea," April gushed behind her.

"Ew. Watch your step," Phoenix warned her when she stepped in something soft and squishy. "That was gross."

She aimed her phone at the floor as they walked, but she swung it back up quickly when she saw the dead rat on the floor.

"Phoenix!"

"C'mon," she urged April. The woman had to be exhausted. It was well after midnight, and her son was missing. Phoenix needed to get her back to the house, give her a cup of tea and maybe a sedative. Anthony would be found. April needed to rest so she was alert when they brought him home.

"Phoenix!" April sobbed.

"What?" Phoenix stopped and looked back over her shoulder. She expected to find April looking at the dead rodent. Instead, April stood frozen, eyes staring into the darkness in the corner of the living room. "What's wrong? What is it? Is someone in here?"

"Look."

Phoenix lifted her phone again, terrified that she would find someone standing in the dark staring back at them. But there was no one. Just a piece of paper on the floor.

"What is it?" she asked April.

The paper was newsprint. The kind she gave the kids to draw on at the church. Phoenix could make out markings on it, but from across the room by the door she couldn't tell what they were. Her stomach twisted as she crossed the room. She recognized the shapes. The child like block letters in the bottom right corner.

Aiming her light at the paper, she squatted down and held her breath, praying nothing would crawl over her feet. She reached with her free hand and turned the paper around right side up. She knew her kids well enough to recognize the artwork. The trees. The church. And a man with big eyes. The trees and the church were drawn in black crayon. The outline of the man was done in what she guessed was apricot, the color kids tended to use to draw people. The man's eyes were red.

"Anthony," she whispered. His name was written in the corner. In his big, block-style print, with the y backwards, the same way he always wrote it, even though she had been working with him to correct that.

Not sure what to do, how to handle April or finding Anthony's drawing in Odell Dunn's house, Phoenix took a deep breath and reminded herself that she had to be calm and get April out of the house first. Behind her,

April sobbed, no doubt imagining the worst about her little boy.

Phoenix mentally chided herself for touching the drawing in case it would be used as evidence, but at least she'd only touched the corner of it. She took a picture of it with her phone, though, with the dirty brown shag carpet and the dingy white wall in the background. Not exactly proof of anything, but still, she felt better as she stood and lunged back across the room. She snatched April's hand again and led her to the door.

Panic stabbed at her as she reached for the doorknob. Had they closed the door all the way? What if it was locked? What if they couldn't get out?

"It's okay," she said out loud, as much for herself as for April. Of course, it was okay. No one had followed them inside. No one had locked them inside. Yes, something was going on if Anthony's drawing was here, but that didn't mean anyone was sneaking around watching them.

When Phoenix pulled the door open, she rushed outside, pulling April behind her, and jumped down the broken concrete stoop.

"Let it go," she told April when the woman turned to pull the door closed.

"What do you think it means?" April swiped at her eyes.

Phoenix figured kids had been messing with Anthony, and that they might have him now. Just to scare him. After all, it was officially Halloween now. But she didn't want to say that to April.

"I don't know." She shook her head. "Let me think."

"Someone took him."

"April, it's probably kids."

"But that doesn't mean it's okay."

"Of course, it's not okay," Phoenix agreed. She took a few steps toward the back of the house.

"No, I mean, kids could hurt him. You see that stuff on the news sometimes."

"We're gonna find him," Phoenix said firmly. She lifted her phone and eyed the tree line behind the shack in the feeble light. A thick oak had crashed into the back of the house, crushing part of the roof. "What's that room? It wasn't the kitchen."

"I need to call Dennis."

"Maybe a back porch," Phoenix said mostly to herself. Someone should probably go back inside and look just to make sure Anthony wasn't there. "Is there a basement?" She wondered aloud as she walked toward the shack.

"Most houses out here just have a crawl space."

Most crawl spaces would be big enough for the body of a four-year-old boy. Phoenix didn't share that thought. No need to throw April into more of a panic.

"Call Dennis. No. Let me call Deputy Webb," Phoenix said quickly. "You said this property backs up to Sapphire Creek?"

April nodded.

"And doesn't the creek dry up just a block or two from the church?"

"Ohmygod!" April wailed.

Phoenix tapped her phone screen, grateful for once that everyone in Ivy knew everyone else in Ivy. She had Caroline Webb's number because the woman wasn't only a sheriff's deputy but a member of the Oakboro Quilting Society. Phoenix had had to call her before about unlocking the sewing room in the church to retrieve a filing cabinet that had been mistakenly moved there.

"Deputy Webb." The woman answered the call instantly, her voice cool and professional. Phoenix had to admire that. As far as she knew, they'd never had a missing child in Ivy. That might shake some people. Caroline Webb apparently had nerves of steel.

"Caroline, it's Phoenix."

"You find something?"

"Maybe."

Phoenix winced when she saw April looking at her own phone. Of course, she would call Dennis. She had to. But Phoenix didn't want to wave a giant red flag and throw everyone into a frenzy, in case this was nothing.

"What is it?"

"April and I are at Odell Dunn's house."

"Why?"

"I don't know. I just wanted to look out here. The kids have been singing that song. I needed to see for myself."

"What'd you find?" Webb's tone brooked no hesitation.

"Someone's been in the house. Windows are all boarded up, but the front door is unlocked. There's some...graffiti inside. More stuff about the devy man."

"Okay. I'll make a note of it."

Maybe she would, but Phoenix hurried to say more before Webb ended the call.

"We found one of Anthony's drawings."

"You did what now?"

"In the living room. It's a...the paper is newsprint. Like I give the kids to draw on. And the drawing is definitely Anthony's. His name is in the corner of the paper."

"Someone put his name on the paper?"

"Anthony did. I know how he writes his name."

Webb sighed.

"On it."

The call ended, and Phoenix looked back to April as she lowered her own phone.

"Dennis is coming."

Phoenix nodded. Deputy Webb hadn't said so, but she imagined someone from the sheriff's office would be here soon, too.

"What we do now?" April's whisper was ragged with tears.

"I guess we wait."

"I can't wait," April argued. "This is my little boy, Phoenix."

Phoenix couldn't begin to know how April felt. A mother's heart lived inside her kids, so she had to be terrified of what was happening right now. Phoenix was scared to death, and she was just Anthony's teacher.

"Okay." She nodded. "Okay. We'll do something."

"The creek."

Phoenix sighed. "First, we need to check that back room. The porch or whatever it is."

April gulped and nodded. "We have to go back inside."

"Let's look around back here and see if there's another door. That way we don't have to go all through the house again."

She had no desire to go back inside that living room. To pass the dead rat. To see the red spray paint in the kitchen. The book about black magic. April followed her as she made her way around the back of the little house. She moved slowly, mindful of the downed tree and the thick undergrowth beneath it. Shattered glass crunched under their feet as they neared the little house again. The roof was caved in under the massive tree, and all three windows back here were broken.

"Careful," Phoenix warned as they stepped up closer to peek in the windows. The room was dark and silent. Phoenix aimed her phone inside again and swept the light around to find more shattered glass and leaves and detritus from the big storm and probably several others since then. April, at the opposite end of the room, held her phone up for more light.

"Anthony?" she called. "Baby, are you in there?"

Her desperation made Phoenix want to vomit.

"There's something on the floor. By the door," April told her.

Phoenix leaned in again to see better.

"Shit!" April hissed and drew her hand away from the window.

"It looks like a pile of rags," Phoenix announced, studying the pile closely to make sure it wasn't a little boy, curled up, afraid and maybe, asleep from exhaustion. "Did you cut yourself?"

"Yes."

Phoenix turned in time to see April sucking on the side of her hand. A natural response, maybe, but Phoenix's urge to scold her was just as natural. The window was filthy. April needed to clean the cut and put an ointment on it. She sure didn't need to put her mouth on it.

"I have some bandages in the car."

"No, I'm fine. Let's just go."

Not surprised by April's insistence that she was fine, Phoenix nodded and turned away from the house. She wished she would have thought to grab a real flashlight before she left her house, but then how could she have known she would find herself clambering around in the woods, walking the creek, looking for Anthony?

They walked for what felt like forever. And yet, Phoenix would bet they hadn't gone a mile. The trees were so thick around Sapphire Creek, little to no moonlight spilled through even the bare branches. What did filter through cast the creek water silver and made the water in the shadows black as night. Again, Phoenix thought about snakes, but again, she pushed the worry from her mind. She had boots and long pants on, so she wasn't likely to get bit. And finding Anthony was the only thing that mattered.

"What did it say?" she asked April now.

"What did what say?" April huffed along beside her, out of breath.

"You said the planchette moved when you and your friend played with the Ouija board. What did it say?"

April didn't answer right away, making Phoenix wonder if she was exhausted or if she had made the story about the Ouija board up.

"Tina asked where the gates of hell were."

"Wow." Phoenix laughed softly. "That's pretty bold."

"Nothing happened then, but she asked if we could speak with a demon."

"Oh God."

"The planchette spelled out yes. At first, I was scared, but then the thing spelled out a name. I got mad. I thought Tina was doing it, so I got mad about it, and we ended up getting in a big fight." April's laugh was cold and bitter. "It blew up into this huge thing that lasted for two years.

Like, that one fight led to both of us just attacking each other all the time. I was really upset, and my mom kept asking me what had happened. So, I finally told her."

"What did she say?"

"That I shouldn't have been playing with a Ouija board." April laughed again. "Tina and I were never the same after that night."

"That sucks," Phoenix mumbled. "But that happens with most friends anyway, right?"

"I guess. She was killed in a car accident about five years ago. I hate that we never set things right again."

They walked on in silence for a few seconds. Phoenix wasn't sure how they would see Anthony even if he was just a step ahead of them.

"What was its name?"

"Olrikath."

"Never heard of it," Phoenix said with a shrug.

"Me neither, but I never forgot it, either."

## 8

Her thighs burned, and her head pounded. Phoenix rubbed at her gritty eyes wishing she was back on the sofa, face smashed in the cushions, sound asleep. And Anthony Hale back in his bed, safe and sound, where he belonged.

"I don't think they'll hurt him," she said softly. April walked beside her, but for a long moment she said nothing.

"Why do you say that?"

Phoenix sighed. She believed it; she wasn't just saying it to keep April going.

"Because we know the kids here, April. This is Ivy, after all. We know *all the kids*. The high school kids. The middle schoolers. Maybe somebody's messed up with drugs, but I can't think of a single kid who would purposely hurt Anthony."

"Sheldon Stevenson."

"Really?" Phoenix shook her head. "Didn't Jovi date him?"

"Yeah. She dumped him for Johnny Reed."

"Hardly reason to scare the bejesus out of her little brother."

"True." April lifted her hand to her face.

"Are you still bleeding?"

"Little bit."

Phoenix figured April was lying, but what could she do about it now? To turn around and head back to Odell Dunn's place, to her SUV parked in front of Odell Dunn's place, would take longer now than it would take them to get to the church.

"Did Jovi say something? To make you think Sheldon would hurt Anthony?"

"No." April sounded sincere this time. "But I'd rather think it's Sheldon than…someone else."

"I know. I get it."

Phoenix considered the teenagers in Ivy. There wasn't one that she could see doing this, but then again, she couldn't imagine any of them torturing and killing animals, either. And Ross had found animal carcasses out by the church the other night.

"Careful," Phoenix warned when she stepped hard and nearly fell up the small incline at the end of the creek. She caught herself with her hand, scraping it on a downed branch. Once she was steady on her feet, she reached back to help April climb up beside her to level ground. "Okay. So, we're close to the church, right?"

"It should be about a block or two to the northeast, I think," April answered.

Phoenix hated the thought of continuing. They were at the end of the creek, but there were still miles of woods ahead of them. And with no creek to lead them in the right direction, their odds of getting lost climbed exponentially higher.

"You okay?" she asked April, maybe to bolster her friend, but maybe as much to keep moving herself.

"Yeah. I just wanna find Anthony."

"Me, too."

Phoenix led the way, with April close on her heels. The moon lit the bare tree branches above them like skeletons reaching from hell for the skies. She thought again of the other night after the Halloween program, losing Anthony, and going out behind the church. That feeling that someone was watching her from the woods.

Some*thing*.

"Your kids don't do that stuff, do they?"

"What stuff?" April asked in a breathy gasp. The terrain in the woods was hard to navigate in the dark. The grass and weeds were tall, and wild plants and bushes shot up everywhere, tripping them and causing them to pitch and stumble forward. Realizing she was moving too fast in her desire to get through the trees, Phoenix slowed a bit for April to catch up. "Drugs?"

"No. Oujia boards."

"Oh God." April groaned. "I don't think so. I mean… Jovi might, I guess. But the boys are still too young, don't you think? To even know what they are?"

"You're kidding, right?" Phoenix asked sarcastically. "There were more kids than adults at the last horror movie I went to."

"Yeah?" April sounded interested. "What movie was it?"

"Um…I don't even know. Maybe *The Conjuring*?"

"So, you'll watch horror movies, but you're afraid of a kid's game?"

"I had a class in Catholicism in college," Phoenix told April. "The priest who taught it said he'd been involved in an exorcism. He also made a convincing warning not to ever invite the occult in."

"So, you believe a Oujia board is a way to speak to spirits? Really?"

"I think if it's possible, why take the chance?" Phoenix shrugged. "And movies aren't real. So, no, they don't bother me."

"Interesting," April decided.

"Look." Phoenix stopped walking so suddenly, April ran into her from behind.

"What?"

"There's the church." She pointed in the general direction of Oakboro Methodist.

"I liked the old church better," April said quietly. "On the other end of town."

"Where was that?"

"They had to tear it down. It was on the flood plain. The Flood of '93? It was just a little old stone building, but it flooded. The whole thing was ruined. The county took it down a year or two later."

"Wow. I knew this was a new building, but I didn't realize the old one flooded."

"Do you see anyone?" April whispered, as if it suddenly occurred to her someone might be watching them.

"No." Phoenix started walking again. "Have you heard from Dennis?"

"No." April slowed again, so Phoenix turned back to her and watched her study her phone screen. Phoenix looked at hers again, noticing she had thirty percent battery left, and it was already nearing two in the morning. Each minute that passed by without finding Anthony was bad.

"Do you have service out here?" Phoenix asked April. She had one bar, so it was possible someone had tried to call, but hadn't been able to get through.

"No."

Before April could move, Phoenix stepped closer and reached for her hand. Blood pooled in her palm. Phoenix took the phone from her and turned it over, shocked at the bloody fingerprints all over the case.

"April!"

"I'm fine. I just need to find Anthony, Phoenix."

"You need stitches."

"I'm fine," April insisted.

Phoenix huffed out a sigh. She thought about calling Caroline Webb again just to check in. But she wanted this search in the woods behind the church over with. She could call Webb when they were done. In fact, she had her keys in her pocket. She and April could go inside the church and wait for Dennis and the sheriff. And Phoenix could clean April's hand up and at least treat her with the first aid kit she kept in her desk.

She walked on, listening to the sounds of April's feet crunching leaves behind her.

"Do you smell that?" She stopped suddenly again. The smell of rotting flesh made her stomach pitch. It was the same thing she had smelled the other night, behind the church.

"April?" she asked when the woman didn't answer her. She turned to look over her shoulder, but April wasn't there. Just trees and the church across the open lot, lit by the moon.

Careful now where she stepped, Phoenix backtracked. Her heartbeat pounded in her throat, in her ears. Had April fallen? Had someone snatched her?

"April?" she called again.

"I'm right here." April's voice sounded muffled. Phoenix lifted her phone and tapped the flashlight app again. She found April about five feet back, half hidden behind a tree. She held onto the tree trunk with her good hand, but she was leaned over, and Phoenix realized she was retching.

"What happened?" Phoenix smoothed her hand over April's back. "Are you okay?"

"Look." April turned her head and swiped her hand over her mouth as she nudged something with the toe of her boot. Phoenix flinched at the dead raccoon at April's feet. Its head had been completely torn away from the body. Phoenix assumed the congealed black spot under the body was blood.

"Yuck." Phoenix looked away and focused on breathing through her mouth.

"Anthony?" April called.

Something mewled in the distance. Phoenix assumed it was a wild animal. Maybe she and April would be lucky enough to run into a coyote out here.

"Anthony?!" April tried again.

Their eyes met in the filmy moonlight. Something was half whining, half howling. And it seemed to be in answer to April's voice.

"Anthony? Is that you?" April called again. "Anthony?"

Nothing.

April stumbled past Phoenix, desperate now to find the owner of the cries. Phoenix scrambled to catch up with her, tripped on a partially exposed tree root, and fell to her knees. With a grunt, she climbed back to her feet and hurried after April, who was still calling out for her son.

"Mommy."

The tiny voice chilled Phoenix. Directly behind the church now, the woods were thick and dark. Phoenix held her breath when she realized this was the spot she would have been staring at the other night, when she felt someone watching her.

"Anthony?" April said again. "Where are you?"

"He said that you would come, Mommy."

"What?"

The light from Phoenix's phone wasn't enough to fight the darkness in this thick copse of trees. Frustrated, she turned in all directions, trying in vain to spot Anthony. Someone started singing. The words were the same that April had recited back at the Hale house at the table with Deputy Webb, but the voice was old and scratchy.

"Anthony?" April called. "Baby, where are you? Let's go home."

"I can't yet, Mommy. You have to talk to him."

"Talk to who, Anthony?"

Phoenix wondered who Anthony could be with out here in the woods. Who would have snuck him out of the house and brought him here to scare him? Or to scare April and Dennis? She still couldn't imagine any of the teens in Ivy doing something so vicious.

"Just talk to him, Mommy," Anthony whispered.

April sobbed and ducked her head like she was in pain.

Suddenly, the woods were lit with fire, and Phoenix felt her heart in her throat again. If the trees out here caught on fire, the whole town of Ivy would go fast.

It was just one flame, though, she realized as she twisted toward the light. April lifted her head to look. She glanced at Phoenix.

"Jesus, April." Phoenix clapped her hand over her mouth, startled to see a drop of black blood just under the woman's nose.

"Let's go, Anthony." April turned back to the flame. Phoenix catalogued the blood all over April's hand. The splotches now on her clothing that had to be from her hand. Why was her nose bleeding? The same way Charlie's had? And Anthony's?

"April."

Phoenix and April both saw the man clearly when he spoke. Tall and lanky, with skin so pale the moonlight reflected off him and painted him silver. His face was pockmarked from scratches, possibly from tree limbs. Possibly from his long, pointed fingernails. He held Anthony by his hair, and even from a distance of five feet, Phoenix could see the grime under his nails and the dirt and dried blood on his hands.

"Who are you?" Phoenix asked him.

"Odell Dunn," April spoke softly, but at the same time, the man's mouth opened to reveal blackened, bloody fangs.

"The body is that of Odell Dunn." His voice was low and thin, but he stepped closer and dragged Anthony with him. Phoenix tore her eyes away from the ghoulish looking face and studied Anthony. Aside from the blood under his nose, he appeared unharmed. He was sock-footed, and he wore thermal pajamas, as if he had been dragged out of bed and to the woods.

April stepped forward and reached for Anthony, but the man twisted sideways to keep him from her reach.

"What are you doing with my son?"

"Sending his soul to hell to brand," the man whispered in a singsong voice. "Because he belongs to me. The devy man."

"The sheriff's right behind us, Odell. I don't care what you're on—"

"Olrikath."

When he spoke, Phoenix shuddered. He looked back at her with glowing red eyes. His fangs grew, as if there was no need to hide any longer. Phoenix felt her stomach roll when he twitched his mouth and sliced a black lip open with his own fang. Blood dribbled over his chin, but a long, black tongue slithered out of his mouth to lick it up.

"What?"

"I've been searching for you, April Hale." The voice was deep and guttural now.

"Let him go, Odell."

For all her fear, her hesitation earlier, April Hale was now a mother whose son had been endangered and was now within her reach.

The man lifted Anthony now as if he weighed no more than a rag doll, his fingers twisted in the boy's hair. He dipped his head toward Anthony and bared a mouthful of fangs.

"No!" April screamed. "No. Please don't hurt him. Please."

"And why shouldn't I?" The man—creature—whatever it was—tipped his head at April curiously. "I've searched for you for years, April Hale. Killed so many just looking for you. Here in Ivy, I finally smelled your blood."

"Who are you?" Phoenix asked again.

The man lifted a hand that now appeared to be more of a cloven hoof than a human claw and motioned as if shoving Phoenix away. She felt the movement in her gut and stumbled backwards several steps, whacking the back of her head on a tree.

"Meddlesome bitch." The eyes glowed again.

Blood ran over Anthony's face, down over his lips and dripped to the ground.

"I smelled your blood, April. And I found your son."

"Let him go."

"I've been watching you."

Phoenix straightened and rubbed the back of her head. The man barely spared her a glance, but Phoenix saw that his hand was just that now. A dirty, skeletal hand with long grimy fingernails.

"I've got his head. I'll steal his brain. I'll roast his body on Samhain. I'll suck his blood and drain him dry. I'll drink his terror when he cries. I'll cast his soul to hell to brand, and he'll belong to the devy man."

The chant, spoken in a menacing whisper, sounded even worse now than when April had recited it at the kitchen table.

Still holding Anthony by the hair, the creature swept his hand over the ground. A fire roared immediately, and flames licked at Anthony's dangling feet. The man—the creature—cast an evil stare at April as he lowered Anthony into the fire.

Phoenix lurched forward, but again, the hand that became a cloven hoof held her off and knocked her back against the tree. Dizzy, overcome with pain, it took her a moment to move this time.

She watched the scene before her, her heart pounding erratically, but unable to stand straight. Her head hurt, and this time, she felt blood trickle down her neck. But she was paralyzed, as if an unseen force held her in place.

Anthony's eyes were closed, and his lips curled in a peaceful smile. But the man—whatever it was—continued to lower the boy into the flames. Phoenix tried to cry out when Anthony's sock caught fire, but she made no sound.

"No!" April screamed and dropped to her knees. "No. Please! Please! Take me."

"Surely you don't mean that. You weren't ready for me the first time we met."

"I do." April sobbed. "I do. Please. Let him go."

Phoenix fell to the ground in a jumble of pain as the man swung Anthony away from the fire and threw him far away into the trees. She held her breath as Anthony's body hit a massive trunk and crumpled to the ground. She struggled to get to her feet, to grab April, so they could run after Anthony and get away.

But the man reached for April and slid his fingers into her hair. He lifted her with ease, just as he had Anthony. April yelped and squirmed, but he held on.

The face changed again until Phoenix found herself staring at something that resembled a man and an animal at the same time. "I am the demon you conjured. I smelled your blood when you were just a child. And now, I've found you, and I have your head, and I'll have your brain. I'll roast your body on Samhain. I'll suck your blood and drain you dry. I'll drink your terror when you cry. I'll cast your soul to hell to brand, and you belong to the devy man."

Phoenix strained to hear sirens. The man-thing cradled a now limp April in his arms. Blood poured from her nose, and he lowered his foul mouth to her face. A loud cry sounded in the woods when that black tongue slithered out to lick the blood from April's face, and Phoenix realized the sound came from her.

She thrashed, trying to move, to save April.

A small sigh slipped from April's lips as the demon lowered his head to nuzzle her neck. Phoenix flinched, her stomach turned, when she heard the crunch of his fangs as he bit into April's neck and tore it apart. Blood poured from the wound and dripped to the ground by the fire. Phoenix managed to lift her hand to cover her mouth. Blood glazed the demon's face as he feasted on her friend. Phoenix prayed that Anthony would not wake up, that he wouldn't come back this way and see what this fiend was doing to his mother.

Finally, the thing lifted his face and met Phoenix's eyes. He smacked his shiny, greasy lips together and ducked his head for more. Long, long minutes later, when April was clearly long dead and her body looked pale in the firelight, the demon dropped her into the flames and danced wildly around the fire as if in celebration.

Phoenix looked again to find Anthony, relieved that he hadn't moved, but worried, too, that he had suffered a head injury when he hit the tree. She swung her gaze back to the creature, afraid that he would come for her next. Still paralyzed, she watched as he continued the dance as he hummed the tune of "Aikendrum."

She needed to vomit. She needed to get to Anthony,

even if she had to crawl all that way over exposed roots and downed limbs and desiccated animal carcasses.

The creature finally stopped the dance and stepped directly into the fire. Phoenix's stomach revolted at the smell of burning flesh. The demon looked at her again, red eyes aglow, and once more began to chant the rhyme about the devy man.

As he finished and the night fell silent other than the crackling of the fire, he descended into the flame until he was gone.

Phoenix watched the fire die slowly, worried that it would burn the town of Ivy to ash. Worried that Anthony Hale might be dead at the base of the tree where he had fallen. Sickened by what she had seen done to April Hale. And afraid that she hadn't seen the last of Olrikath.

# EPILOGUE

Deputy Webb told Phoenix they found her in the woods, awake but dazed and confused, mumbling Halloween mumbo-jumbo about demons and fires. Apparently, the sheriff had sent a small group to Odell Dunn's shack in response to Phoenix's call. Deputy Webb, herself, had found Anthony's artwork in the building, which had prompted a bigger response. The sheriff abandoned his position at the Hale home, turned his lights on, and raced to County Road 669E. They'd searched the shack and found more empty liquor bottles and cigarette butts, but according to Webb, no conclusive evidence of anything, not even that kids had been using the shack as a party house.

When more deputies found April's blood on the shattered window glass, Dennis had insisted on following Sapphire Creek to look for both his son and his wife. Instead, Dennis had found Phoenix, Webb found the decapitated racoon that had made April ill, and Reverend

Tweedy had been the hero to see Anthony's lifeless body at the base of a massive tree.

Anthony would make a full physical recovery. Both he and Phoenix had been taken to the ER in Jester. Phoenix was grateful that she could sit beside him in the exam room and comfort him while Dennis dealt with the red tape of insurance and hospital visits. Anthony had suffered two broken ribs and a broken arm. Phoenix had worried about a concussion, but his torso had taken the brunt of the hit.

When Sheriff Baxter and Deputy Webb questioned Phoenix later, after she'd had what they thought was plenty of rest—it wasn't, because her sleep had been plagued with dreams of fire and blood—she claimed she didn't know what had happened to April. That she had fallen and bumped her head on an exposed tree root. She had enough cuts and bruises for the story to be believable, but she knew from the way they watched her as she spoke that they knew she was holding back.

Once they were gone, she whispered the whole story to Dennis Hale. After all, he deserved to know the truth. His wife hadn't left him. She hadn't run off because she was desperate or wrecked over losing her son. She had fought for her little boy and sacrificed herself in the end, and Phoenix wanted Dennis to know that.

Also, Phoenix believed Dennis should know what had happened to his wife, because he should know who or what had taken his son. He didn't want to believe her; Phoenix didn't blame him. It was a crazy story from beginning to end. And yet, April had left a trail of blood and then vanished into thin air in the woods behind the church.

Phoenix worried that Anthony might need counseling or therapy. Even if he hadn't seen the demon tear his mother's throat out and then drop her in the fire, he had been taken from his room. An evil entity had haunted him for days and then taken him from his room and dragged him through the woods as bait to get his mother.

Phoenix and Dennis agreed that Anthony needed time before he returned to preschool, if he did return at all. He might benefit from the socialization there, and the curriculum Phoenix taught wouldn't hurt him. But he was prepared for kindergarten whether or not he finished the year with her.

Still, the Hale family was important to Phoenix and Lynnea, so Phoenix continued home visits just to check on Anthony. To check on the rest of the family. Aiden and the other two boys seemed unfazed, though obviously they all missed April, but Jovi was twitchy and restless. Losing April had wrecked Dennis, but Phoenix was relieved to see him trying harder to be present for his children. Whenever she dropped in on them, she found him in the kitchen cooking dinner or trying to help with homework, and if he was working, Jovi had picked up the slack.

"What're your plans for Thanksgiving?" she asked him now. Dennis, both hands hidden in oven mitts, looked at her from the stove across the small kitchen.

"We'll have dinner at my brother's house. Most of the family will be there."

Phoenix nodded, pleased to hear that Dennis wouldn't be suffering through the holiday on his own with his kids.

"Is Jovi doing okay?"

"I s'pose." He pulled the oven door open and reached

in for a casserole dish. Phoenix knew neighbors and family were still dropping food items off for him and the kids. "She spends a lot of time in her room now."

Phoenix didn't remind him that Jovi was a teenager and probably spent a lot of time in her room before things had gone to hell.

"Do you wanna stay for dinner?" he offered.

She didn't. She wasn't hungry. She hadn't been able to eat much since Halloween, and besides, it was one thing to drop in and check on the Hales. But she couldn't linger, because time spent around Anthony, around the house, triggered nightmares of her own.

She couldn't remember things clearly now. She knew something strange had happened in the woods behind the church. She knew she'd been less than forthcoming with the sheriff and Deputy Webb about what she had seen, just as she knew she'd confided the whole story to Dennis when they were alone. Beyond that, she didn't know.

But her nightmares were terrifying. Images of fire. Some kind of demon creature that she'd apparently seen in a movie. Physical pain that left her paralyzed in her sleep but vanished when she awoke.

"No. Thank you, though." She started to stand, but Anthony jumped down the stairs and appeared suddenly in the kitchen. "Hey, Anthony. How are you?"

"Hi Miss Phoenix." The kid flashed her a sweet smile.

"What've you been up to?"

"Jovi reads to me," he answered, and he puffed his chest up to continue, "and she taught me words to read."

"That's great, Anthony!" Phoenix twisted her chair around as he slinked closer to her and climbed into her lap. His sweaty-doughy little boy scent was familiar to her, and for a moment, it made her think of April. She swallowed down a knot of emotion and turned her attention to the paper he spread out before her on the table. "Did you draw something new?"

"Yes." He flattened the newsprint out with his chubby little hands. When he tipped his head to look at her, Phoenix drew her gaze away from his dirty hands, shuddering at the thick black dirt under his fingernails.

"What is it?" She looked from his big brown eyes to the paper, uncertain what she was looking at. "Tell me about your picture."

"It's like a telephone," he told her.

Phoenix studied the row of letters at the top of the paper, some capitalized, some lowercase, some little more than scribbles and some backwards.

"You mean like a computer? Like a keyboard?" she asked him as she narrowed her eyes and studied the picture.

"No. It's a way to call him," Anthony insisted. "You put your hand here." At this, he put his hand on a triangle in the middle of the paper and looked back at her. "And you call him. And he answers with this."

The hair on the back of her neck raised. She hadn't felt this way, as if someone was watching her, in a while. Not since—

"Call who, Anthony?"

"The devy man, Miss Phoenix!" Anthony's mouth curved up in a grin.

## ACKNOWLEDGMENTS

Thank you to my writer bestie, Kate Carley, for reading *The Devy Man*, even when it's not your genre. It's so awesome to have a friend like you to bounce ideas off of and to plot with. So happy we met in Minnesota at the MBLU and I'm so thankful to call you my friend.

## ABOUT THE AUTHOR

Tracy is the author of the Lorelei Bluffs women's fiction series, the Williams Legacy, and several stand-alone women's fiction novels. She has recently dabbled in contemporary romance, as well.

## ALSO BY TRACY BROEMMER

Also by Tracy Broemmer

Women's Fiction Novels:

Luther's Cross (Writing as Therese Kinkaide)

Luther's Cross 10th Anniversary Edition (Tracy Broemmer)

Fairytale (Writing as Therese Kinkaide)

Just Like Them (Writing as Therese Kinkaide)

Small Hours (Writing as Therese Kinkaide)

Picket Fences

Two Story Home

Green-Eyed Girl

Say Everything

Come Home For Christmas

Sketching Litchfield Lake

Ever, Again

Safe as Houses

Damsel

Every Little Thing, Lorelei Bluffs, Book 1

Two A.M., Lorelei Bluffs, Book 2

Blind, Lorelei Bluffs, Book 3

Leaving July, Lorelei Bluffs, Book 4

Hesitation Marks, Lorelei Bluffs, Book 5

Four Letter Words, Lorelei Bluffs, Book 6

See Kate, Lorelei Bluffs, Book 7

Loved You More, Lorelei Bluffs, Book 8

A Lorelei Ending, Lorelei Bluffs, Book 9

I Do, Lorelei Bluffs, Book 10

Truth Is, The Williams Legacy, Book 1

Other People's Ugly, The Williams Legacy, Book 2

Omissions, The Williams Legacy, Book 3

Contemporary Romance Novels:

Destiny's Calling: Your Future Is Waiting

Wedding Day Shenanigans

Holiday Fling

The Kiss Off

Something Like Love

Love, Nashville, The Mississippi Queen Trilogy, Book 1

Forever, Duncan, The Mississippi Queen Trilogy, Book 2

Always, Jess, The Mississippi Queen Trilogy, Book 3

Getting' Hitched, The H Books, Book 1

Contemporary Romance Novellas:

Indian Summer, A Novella

Dear Jaclyn Perris, A Novella

French Stuff, A Novella Published in Just Coffee Anthology

Boone's Girl, A Novella Published in Aced Anthology

Contemporary Romance Short Stories:

Perfect Pictures, The Wine Tasting Series, Traminette

Coming Home, The Wine Tasting Series, Edelweiss

Save Me Every Dance, The Wine Tasting Series, Rosé

Marry Me, The Wine Tasting Series, Shiraz

Birthday Wishes, The Wine Tasting Series, Muscat

Dad Jeans, The Wine Tasting Series, Vignoles

www.ingramcontent.com/pod-product-compliance
Lightning Source LLC
Chambersburg PA
CBHW020417130626
46549CB00006B/2606